Jacks and ~~Knaves~~

by
Adam Parish

Book 5 of the
Jack Edwards and Amanda Barratt
Mystery Series

Also by Adam Parish
The Quartermaster (1)
Parthian Shot (2)
Loose Ends (3)
Business as Usual (4)

To sign up for offers, updates
and find out more about Adam Parish
visit our website www.adam-parish.com

Thanks to Helen for her
help, humour, and patience,
Fran, Sandy, Tom and Hamish
for their ideas and time
and Mandy for everything

Chapter 1

Was there no such thing as a single girl in this town?

He slugged down some Guinness, but that tasted sour now. Maybe he had hit the wall? No; he rallied and won a battle by turning a potentially humiliating wave of nausea into a single hiccup.

The bar was packed. Laughter and companionship everywhere, except at his solitary table.

Then he saw her. All on her own. How was that possible?

He creased his face into a smile. That was usually good enough. Bingo.

Speak properly. Don't slur your words. "Drink?"

She smiled in assent.

Through a haze of cigarette smoke, he battled to the bar. A long wait. He looked round. She was still there. Still smiling.

Careful now. A slight misstep, but she didn't notice him spilling a little beer over a carpet that no longer cared.

He never really knew how he did it, but he always did.

Words were exchanged. Meaningless words.

Her head gently swayed from side to side. "This place is getting on my nerves. Let's go."

After the stifling atmosphere of the saloon, the street air was sharp and cold. Steadily falling rain formed a thin film across his face. The woman took his arm and led him along the dark street, then through a series of narrow lanes, which cut through the blocks of black terraced houses.

It was a funny old town. Less than half a mile from the city centre, the silence was absolute.

Yet another lane. Darker, narrower than the others. The brick wall recessed and she pulled him in.

She held him close. Her lips exploded into his.

Nothing mattered now. Nothing but her. Not the faint sound over the freshening breeze. Not even the nagging certainty of gathering footsteps.

Through the gloom, a black, hooded figure fell heavily onto his knees only feet from them, breathing urgently. The newcomer recovered quickly and turned towards them. Maybe he was going to say something?

The sky filled with blinding white light, whiter and brighter than he had ever seen. Violent ejaculations from an automatic weapon.

The newcomer lay motionless. Through over-sized eyeholes in the balaclava, the eyes were open and staring heavenward at the single star that pierced the night sky.

His first dead body. Fascinating for a second or two. Then he violently recoiled and vomited until he had emptied the contents of his stomach.

Blackness and silence, then footsteps.

He moved out from the recess and picked up the newcomer's fallen gun.

The footsteps had stopped now.

He turned. In front of him, partially illuminated by an intermittent street lamp, the fresh face of a boy stared. He was about seventeen years old, wore khaki, and his helmet was too big. Probably he had passed basic training, but that was about all.

The boy's rifle rose.

The man hadn't had any basic training, just five minutes of action of a sort.

Flight was impossible. Hello, death.

Instinctively he pulled the trigger of the handgun. The boy in the big helmet fell to the ground, the end of another mother's son. He took a step towards the body but was arrested by the firm grip on his arm.

"This way."

Chapter 2

Particles of stoor danced excitedly in a long, sunlit beam that intruded through the narrow opening between the pair of flowery curtains. The breath of a zephyr flowed idly below the sill of the window; its gentle thrusts danced along the curtains and sometimes pushed beams of light across the face of the solitary figure who lay in the single bed.

David Ross returned to life and slowly opened his heavy eyelids. The omnipresent sterile scent of disinfectant hit him. The room was exactly as he remembered it from an hour or two ago. Every day was the same, punctuated with numerous deep but short sleeps and, every time he awoke, the hope of renewal or, in his darker moments, death.

He didn't feel all that sick today, so he tried to raise himself up in the bed. Beads of sweat forming on his forehead reminded him of the truth.

He relapsed from the exhausting effort of failing to sit up and decided that today, on balance, he was happy still to be alive. Exactly why, he didn't know; he just was. He glanced at his wristwatch. Twenty-nine minutes past four. He hoped it wasn't; maybe his viewing angle was deceptive. If he was right, this was unpalatable news, for it meant the imminent arrival of the punctual and efficient Nurse Lewis, who would certainly, whether requested or otherwise, attend to his every need.

Even writing was a struggle now, but every day he somehow managed. Just a few more words. Ross picked up his two booklets, reached across to the small bedside cupboard, put them in and locked it.

The door opened and the dreaded Nurse Lewis arrived. She paused at the wash-hand basin, and although it had certainly not been used since her last microscopic inspection, pored over the porcelain and its appendages. She straightened one of the towels, then walked briskly across to the floral curtain and, without consideration, yanked the curtains open.

Ross narrowed his eyes to counter the light. Miss Lewis wasn't cruel, just certain that some things were right, others were wrong, and from her personal canons there could be neither compromise nor deviation. She continued with her well-rehearsed routine, moving her attention to the bedside table and the decanter. She removed the stopper and poured half a glass of rather old and stale-looking water. She then delved into her pocket, produced his afternoon preparation and handed it and the water to him.

It seemed to help, for a second later he discovered sufficient strength to lift himself up a little more and she, a woman who would help someone if she believed that they were trying to help themselves, cooperated by propping up the pillows.

Lewis was a sexless creature of uncertain age. Her hair was dark, short without a discernible style, and her face, although not unpleasant, had a neutral and lifeless appearance.

She was leaning across him reordering the bedclothes, and for a moment she was very close to him. Her cheek brushed his nose, and as she reached for the most remote and recalcitrant bedsheet edge, her breasts pressed hard into his chest, which did so little to restore Ross's senses that it annoyed him further.

He was three-quarters dead and he knew it.

Nurse Lewis restored herself to her full height, and after spending further unnecessary time wandering about the room inspecting and correcting nothing in particular, she finally stopped and sat down in the wooden chair that was paired with the writing desk.

She sometimes did this, but not very often, and Ross was never sure what prompted her.

He never really enjoyed their little chats anyway, in which she contributed little and never expressed an opinion, preferring instead blandishments such as 'life's like that'.

"How are you feeling today, Mr Ross?"

In the beginning he had once asked her to call him David. She had refused, and he had never raised the subject again. It was now their guilty secret.

"A little better."

She accepted this obvious lie in her stride and said, "Good," and added, "I think that the new medication's a distinct improvement."

Ross contributed a low grunt of assent and Lewis seemed satisfied, for she got up and said, "Good. I think that's enough talking. Time for a sleep." Then she was gone.

Ross considered the short, meaningless conversation and another opportunity wasted. He longed for her to say something about life beyond this hospital or even beyond this room. Next time he would force the issue. He considered his alternatives. He could ask her something about the form of his favourite football team, but he knew she would have nothing to say. Or perhaps a political argument; now, that would be fun.

Or maybe he should go for the jackpot. Women were not really Ross's cup of tea. What would be the right words? Maybe an off-colour remark next time she leant across him? She might be forced into letting her mask slip. Be outraged and appalled. If he was lucky, maybe she would slap his face.

No. He couldn't do that. Not that he was put off by the remote chance that she might be offended. Rather the reverse – the small risk that she would exhibit signs of life and react. He knew he wouldn't be able to stand that. Ross had given up on life, and to be reminded of its joys, even its frustrations, was now too painful for him to bear.

Chapter 3

An overworked fan and open windows were no defence against the searing heat of a central London summer afternoon. Patrick Lawrence clicked his mouse idly through the various games and other meaningless accessories of his desktop.

As an investigative journalist, Lawrence was on a roll, but it was a poor one. The extended honeymoon of the new government had meant very little by way of gossip, stories and other tittle-tattle, serious or otherwise. No embittered MPs with dashed careers to provide some major schism for him to exploit and, worse, the public couldn't give a toss.

Ungrateful bastards, thought Lawrence as he finally lost enthusiasm for the game and released the mouse. He fell into his chair, pushed it back from the desk, leant back and put his feet atop it. His beard, three or so days old, was now annoying him. He needed a story and he needed one soon.

He shut his eyes and forced himself to think. A promising start lasted a full five seconds before it was interrupted by a blast from his mobile. He swore and looked at the offender resentfully, then, after a number of rings, answered it. Maybe it was something interesting?

It wasn't. The unmistakeable coarse Scottish tones of Gus McWhirter came through clear and very loud. McWhirter was a relic. More than a relic. He had last been "on message" in about 1970, probably not even then. It was as if the cultural revolution in the west had never taken place. On the "wrong" side of every social issue, a fact he never sought to deny, it was incredible that he endured. McWhirter possessed many other unappealing qualities, not least of which was the fact that he was Lawrence's editor and boss.

That the telephone was for a message and not a conversation was a maxim that McWhirter subscribed to. With exactly eight words, which included two swear words but neither a salutation nor farewell, McWhirter invited Lawrence to join him in his office.

Lawrence slammed down the phone. He was an independent man. McWhirter could wait.

After a couple of seconds, he got up wearily and, passing a number of working journalists, languidly headed to McWhirter's office.

McWhirter was working too, engaged in conversation with two telephones, one at either ear. His office smelt stale and the atmosphere was more stifling than the main office, without concession nor relief from an open window. McWhirter, however, thrived on heat and was sporting a shirt, tie and, incredibly, a sports jacket. Lawrence felt hot just looking at him. In response to a wave of McWhirter's hand, he slumped into a chair in the manner of one whose heart wasn't really in it – which it wasn't.

Lawrence looked up at McWhirter, who, unusually, was still on the phone and was smiling. He might, after all, be human. It was just possible, supposed Lawrence, that somewhere within, although very deeply hidden, there lived a warm and vulnerable human being.

McWhirter was bald and considerably shorter than his weight demanded. Lawrence thought that he was on the wrong side of sixty, but beyond that he was not prepared to guess. He lived for his work and never seemed to age, but Lawrence knew that when it was all over, McWhirter would be too.

As always, McWhirter's tone and words failed to alert the listener that the conversation was about to be terminated. With no obvious valediction, McWhirter ended both calls, put his hands behind his head and leant back in his high-backed executive chair.

At first he said nothing, but regarded Lawrence with what would have looked, to an outsider, as a hostile eye. It was, in fact, nothing more than one of McWhirter's favoured opening conversational gambits.

Lawrence waited.

McWhirter's voice, when it came, was in calm and measured Highland Scottish tones. "Well, Paddy, how's things going?"

Lawrence gave a languid shrug of his shoulders and then admitted, "Quiet."

"Aye, son, that's the very word for it, quiet," McWhirter repeated. He added wistfully, "Not like when I was a laddie. There was always plenty happening then." He looked skyward, as if revelling in warm, sweet memories of ages past.

Lawrence knew not to interject at this point and that meaningless comparative exchanges upon journalism since the Stone Age would not be McWhirter's ultimate destination.

"Mind you, son, there were times when it wasnae always on a plate for us either, so…" he added, looking paternalistically, "we had to get off our arses and dig up something."

The pause was shorter this time, as McWhirter sped to his denouement. He said, more with sadness than sarcasm, "Still, no point living in the past. We cannae expect you lazy young bastards to get on with it yourselves, can we, eh?"

Lawrence smiled weakly and watched as McWhirter made exaggerated searching movements through the debris on the desk before emerging triumphantly with a single sheet. "Ah, here it is."

Lawrence forced himself out of his chair, took the sheet and appraised its contents. It didn't take long. "Sheila Cahill", followed by a number.

Failing to conceal his disinterest and disappointment, Lawrence said, "Aw fuck, is this what it's come to? Fetching and carrying for the government?"

McWhirter shrugged. "Maybe, but have you got anything else on?"

Lawrence shrugged. There was no denying he'd had a lean period. "You know her?"

Lawrence did. "Sheila Cahill, member of parliament. Cabinet minister without portfolio. The spin doctor's spin doctor – ruthless and ambitious. They say she won the election."

"Nasty bitch, that Cahill lassie. She'd never have gotten within a hundred miles of Whitehall in my day." McWhirter added thoughtfully, "A fuckin' horror, too." He then explained, with hand gestures, what he looked for in a woman.

Lawrence risked an interruption this time. If not, McWhirter would find his form and kick off a long and oft-told anecdote about how his poor mother was twice the woman the likes of Cahill would ever be, arguing that no calling could stand above raising a family of six.

"Well, what's the deal? Have you any idea what Cahill wants?"

McWhirter shrugged. "Fucked if I know. She phoned and asked for you. Said she'd only speak to you. She mentioned some of your political exclusives. She must have a good memory."

Lawrence let this criticism go. It was a fair comment really.

"Well, anyway, give her a ring – you've got nothing else to do. See what she wants. There might be something in it. And," McWhirter added, "shave that fucking beard off."

Lawrence was all out of excuses, so without further comment returned to his message-free desk, where he carelessly deposited the communication and considered his first move.

Time for a drink. He deliberated between the respective attractions of the Griffin and the White Horse, two of his favourite and filthiest haunts. He had patronised the White Horse yesterday, so, he argued, it was only reasonable to favour the Griffin today. This major decision taken, he rose swiftly and headed out of the office with enthusiastic and purposeful strides.

Then a funny thing happened, and he found himself returning to his desk and picking up his mobile. After three or four rings, the phone spoke with the familiar tones of the government's de-facto chief information spokesman. "Sheila Cahill here. How can I help?"

"It's Patrick Lawrence from the Tribune. I heard you were trying to reach me."

"Oh yes, Mr Lawrence, thanks for calling. Could we meet? I think I've got something that will interest you."

No doubt you fucking have, thought Lawrence. Well, if he must play the patsy, then he must. "Okay. Where and when?"

"Do you know Somerville's, just off Holborn?"

There wasn't a bar in central London that Lawrence didn't know. Somerville's was a strange choice: an unfashionable bar and brasserie rarely patronised by high-powered politicians.

"Yeah, I know it."

"Good. Can you manage seven tonight?"

"Let me see," he said, consulting his virgin diary. "Yes, fine."

The appointment was agreed. He already regretted making it. It was just past three and the Griffin awaited.

Chapter 4

Patrick Lawrence glanced at the clock on the wall. Ten minutes before the meeting. Time for another.

Lawrence's mood had worsened by the time he arrived at the restaurant some thirty minutes late, having spent a frustrating time being ignored by all of the capital's cab drivers, hence being forced to jog the entire route.

The restaurant was upmarket and service immediate, in the form of two well-dressed and zealous attendants. He squared off the first with his coat then turned to the other. "A booking in the name of Cahill?"

The waiter scanned the book rapidly. "Sorry, sir, nothing in that name."

Good. Hopefully she had better things to do. He certainly had, but professionalism demanded that he ask again. He spelled out the name.

"Sorry, sir. I can get you a table, but it might be about half an hour?"

He scanned the busy restaurant for what he hoped would be the last time. She wasn't there. "No, no thanks, my mistake."

Lawrence made to leave but managed only a half-turn. Cahill was beside him, a tallish thin woman with very light and wispy brown shoulder-length hair, which did nothing to detract from her hard features. He had met her once or twice but not for some time, and, to his surprise, she was, if anything, even uglier than he remembered.

Despite this, she didn't lack confidence. She was standing very close, staring up at him through her hazel eyes. Then, with alarming over-familiarity, she took his hand and led him to a table set back in a small dimly lit alcove.

They sat down. A waiter arrived with drinks. He did not remember ordering a drink. If there was one thing worse than a control freak, it was a control freak who got it right. He took a long mouthful of whisky and water.

She sipped tight-lipped at what looked like a glass of mineral water.

She was looking hard at him and he was doing his best to avoid her gaze, but she seemed able to tough it out a bit longer.

"Now, let's see, when was it we last met?" She thought for a little and answered her own question. "It must have been just before the election was called. And then …" She smiled again. "There was that time at the party conference. You asked me some tough questions."

He vaguely remembered and nodded with fake enthusiasm.

"What have you been doing since then?"

"Oh, this and that."

She continued in her most emollient tone, "Working on some exposé – about to embarrass us?" She then emitted a short, high-pitched sound, almost a giggle. He broke her gaze and focused on his now empty whisky tumbler. She didn't say anything, so he looked at her again. The soft lighting hadn't improved her looks, but her face looked different now, a little softer. A look that Lawrence was not unfamiliar with – she was definitely flirting with him.

"Why did you ask for me?"

"You made a big impression on me the last time we met." She cracked a big smile and let him enjoy it before continuing. "I need someone of experience and ability for this job. You've broken some big stories. So naturally, I thought of you."

He ignored these compliments and decided to play her game. He hailed a waiter and ordered another drink, leant forward in his seat, softened his expression and held her gaze.

He took a small sip of his whisky. "Well, Sheila." He paused to see what reaction the use of her first name would have. She smiled again. She liked it. "To tell you the truth, there's not been a lot happening recently. In fact, I was hoping you would have something good for me. Although" – and he dropped his voice in preparation for the big lie – "it's good to see you again anyway." Lawrence was pretty accomplished at this sort of talk but even he was having trouble being sincere; it seemed to be working, though, and now she was almost purring.

He said, tapping her half empty glass, "Don't you ever have a proper drink?"

"Well," she teased, "only on special occasions."

"Okay then, what'll it be?"

She dropped her eyelashes and said archly, "You choose for us both."

Lawrence decided to make them doubles.

More smiles were exchanged, but little conversation. Mercifully, the drinks arrived quickly and she returned to business. "Patrick, now, the reason I asked to meet with you was because I've got some pretty interesting information. From your point of view, it's a career-changer, but I've got to be sure you are someone I can trust." She looked at him and in low conspiratorial tones said, "Can I trust you, Patrick?"

"Of course, I'm a journalist."

She laughed this off mirthlessly. "Before we get into the details, I want you to know that I believe in my government and want to do all I can to help it succeed." She tried her whisky cautiously and added, "But for us to succeed there must be no distractions and we've got to get rid of the weak links."

"Weak links?" he repeated. His heart sank. So this was it. A smear campaign against some cabinet colleague. A political innocent who would have committed no crime other than to go "off message" or, even worse, to have the courage of conviction and express a personal opinion. Lawrence was sick and tired of being used but too tired to care. For all he knew, whoever Cahill was about to brief against might deserve it. So, he waited as she went on.

"Patrick, as I say, this requires careful handling. Now, off the record to start with and the usual 'unattributable sources'," she said, emphasising the last words unnecessarily.

He nodded again. Would she ever come to the point?

She cleared her throat deliberately and moved her face a little nearer. "Basically, the fact is that I have become privy to some concerning information about the prime minister."

It was a decent opening hook and Lawrence, despite himself, was interested.

"Adam Chandler is a great prime minister and he has done so much for our party, and the country of course. However, it seems that he has been leading a secret private life, and the facts indicate many lovers and a trail of, what we might call, risky relationships." She lowered her voice and added, with illiberal emphasis, "Men and women, Patrick."

Lawrence had to work hard to stop his head shaking or a laugh escaping. "Maybe thirty years ago."

"Surely nothing sells like a good old-fashioned sex scandal?"

He shrugged. "Not so much nowadays."

"There's a lot more than that. There was also an incident with a former secretary."

"It happens."

"A difference of opinion over the meaning of the word consensual."

"I never heard about that."

"That's what you should expect to hear when I cover something up, Patrick."

"Impressive."

"Not really. It's amazing how people become persuaded after a chat with our private investigators and a little money. And, of course, the possible loss of reputation."

"Lucky for you she didn't keep her little black dress," Lawrence retorted.

This earned a thin flickering smile from Cahill, who continued, "That's all history. The key thing is that I now know he is being blackmailed by one of his many former lovers and" – she paused before the punchline – "he is preparing to pay him off. Not just with money, but also with government favours. And it's not the first time."

"How do you know all this? "

She laughed casually. "Just one of these strange things that came out of the blue. Something that no one else really appreciated. An irrelevant bit of hate mail delivered to party headquarters. I mean, we get dozens of these daily."

"I expect you do," Lawrence said ambiguously.

"Normally, I would have ignored it also, but I decided to do a little investigating."

"Why?"

"Oh, some of us just have a nose for these things."

"Can't you share a little bit more?" Lawrence asked.

"Soon, Patrick."

"When was this note delivered?"

"About a month ago."

"Who delivered the note?"

Cahill sighed. "It was hand-delivered by an insignificant little man from Paddington – McMahon or something. Apparently he was reeking of alcohol. Could hardly walk straight. But he's not important. He's a drug addict and was just peddling a bit of gossip, trying to make a quick buck. What is important is what I did next in following this up. I have uncovered an incredible and very serious state of affairs."

"All that from one insignificant note?"

"McMahon had other contacts and, anyway, a lot of work led to the story."

"Who?"

"Just be patient."

"Okay," Lawrence said, "you say this note went to party headquarters. Surely others know about this?"

"The party chairman Patterson and his deputy knew about the note – it was addressed to the chairman but he dismissed it as a joke and didn't follow it up." She laughed, "Fools." She indicated a bulging buff folder. "Everything's in this file. Details of numerous corrupt deals, affairs and favours."

Lawrence moved his hand towards the folder.

Cahill brushed it off playfully. "All in good time, Patrick. If we can work out a way to work together, I'll share everything with you."

"But why would you want this out in the open?"

She sat up taller and her eyes widened." No one's above our cause, Patrick, not even the prime minister."

"And if Chandler goes?"

"We'll need a new leader."

"There will be many candidates."

"Of course, but really it's about who the sponsors of the party back."

"Who do you think they'll back?"

A faint smile broke across Cahill's face. "I already know who they back."

"Have you spoken to them?"

"Meetings are arranged."

Lawrence said, "When?"

Cahill stared. "Very soon, Patrick. Take my word for it – Adam Chandler will be out in a week."

"That's a bold claim."

She stood up, the buff folder under her arm. "One week, that's a promise."

Lawrence exhaled powerfully. His heart was thumping. He watched her walk to the bathroom. Were her hips swinging? Maybe, but Lawrence was more interested in her story.

Cahill was compelling, supremely confident. That folder was thick. He hated to admit it, but McWhirter had been right. Cahill was a caricature: a nightmarish male vision of a power-crazy modern female, seemingly carrying the torch for women everywhere but, in reality, carrying a torch only for herself. He couldn't work out either why such careerism, naked ambition and narcissism, all traits so common in men, were so repellent when embodied in a woman.

He didn't know the answer to this, so he settled for a careless review of the menu, but he couldn't stop thinking about what was inside that folder. There was just a chance that this was the story of the decade, and if he played this right, it was all his.

Great news should always be conveyed quickly. Lawrence called his boss.

Chapter 5

Jack Edwards was a creature of habit and preferred not to be prised from his solitary life in his Scottish Highland home without a good reason. Sitting in a bar in a hotel in an unremarkable part of Essex was not a good reason, but meeting up with Amanda Barratt was. He had no idea what she wanted and he hadn't asked. He could argue about that later.

Right now, he was thinking about Amanda the woman, not the maverick British spy. He had been thinking about her quite a lot recently. As a prospective partner, Amanda was quite a catch. Her job was a problem, but this apart, she was brainy, accomplished and beautiful and, most of all, had a grand gift of knowing how much time together was enough. Most would say he was punching way above his weight. That was probably true, but he had never felt it. How like a man.

He fiddled with the remains of a gin and tonic and looked across the nondescript and unpatronised bar. This level of demand looked satisfactory to the young, long-haired, white-shirted barman who loitered within a small annex reading a newspaper. Jack didn't want another drink but decided to disturb him.

With weary reluctance, close to maturing to sullenness, the barman approached Jack. "Yes, sir, what can I get for you?"

"Another gin, double please."

The youthful barman fixed the drink but did not return to his retreat and stood, arms folded, facing Jack as if expecting conversation, although volunteering none.

Jack had no stomach for even routine insincere pleasantries and returned to his seat, and the barman returned to his newspaper. For several minutes both parties maintained their silent poses, until the opening of the bar door broke the moment.

It was a woman of maybe thirty. Nice looking, but not Amanda.

She was interesting enough to catch the barman's attention, and his nonchalance was replaced with an alert and over-familiar smile.

In the absence of background music, Jack listened in.

In a soft, refined but assertive voice she said, "Vodka and tonic, please." She turned to scan the room and flashed Jack a polite smile, while the barman unfroze and moved to execute the commission.

Once in receipt of her drink, she again looked around at the endless empty tables and then headed towards Jack. "Hello. It seems to be just us. Can I join you?"

"Yes, of course," Jack said nervously.

She offered her hand. "Ray Dewar."

"Jack Edwards."

"Nice to meet you, Jack. Are you here on business?"

Jack really didn't know why he was there, so he had a better look at Ray Dewar instead. About thirty, he thought. Her short thick hair was flaming red, naturally curly and was cut in no discernible style. Her eyes were large and green, and her face was fresh and rustic looking. He said vaguely, "Oh just here for the day. You?"

"Same."

Jack couldn't think of anything else to say. "Can I get you a drink?"

"No, I've hardly started this one. Besides, I'm driving back to London later."

The conversation was already flagging, but then the bar door opened again. A moment later, Amanda was standing alongside.

Amanda didn't look at him at first but instead gave his new friend a rapid appraisal. Having done so, she turned to him.

Jack said, "Hello, this is Ray, Ray Dewar," and added, "Amanda Barratt."

Amanda said, "Pleased to meet you, Ray."

"Do you want a drink?" he asked Amanda.

"No time. Dinner's in about thirty minutes. We need to get ready."

Normally Jack took about thirty seconds to get ready for dinner, but as he was here at Amanda's invitation he could hardly demur, so he got up and said, "Well, nice to meet you, Ray. Perhaps we'll run into each other again?"

Ray Dewar smiled and nodded, and Jack followed Amanda out of the bar. Against his better judgement, he allowed himself a look back. He wondered if she'd be staring, love-struck, after him, but she wasn't, preferring to work through a broadsheet newspaper.

Jack followed Amanda up two flights of stairs and into a surprisingly well-appointed double room, spacious enough to include a small living area with a low table and a couple of comfortable-looking armchairs.

"Do you want some coffee?" Amanda asked.

"Yes, thanks."

She fixed two mugs and sat on the opposite armchair.

Jack smiled at her. "Nice to see you."

She smiled back, "Sorry to take you away from Ms Dewar. A friend of yours?"

"No, afraid not. We were just chatting."

Amanda laughed. "Seems I can't leave you alone in a hotel bar."

Jack protested. "It was her who sat beside me."

"Did no one tell you about Essex girls?"

"I don't know anything about Essex girls, or any girls really. Besides, she wasn't from Essex. Quite well-spoken actually."

Amanda tested her coffee and smiled. "So, just your type."

"I don't have a type."

"What about late thirties, brunette, spy?"

"Well maybe, but why are we out in the wilds of Essex?"

"Why not? I haven't heard from you for months. I thought you might be bored and could do with a change of scene?"

"Well, that's true enough," he admitted

Her expression changed and she stopped smiling. "How have you been?"

"Okay, I suppose. Not too active. Although I have finished the library, at last. And I've been doing a bit of exercise."

"Cigarettes?"

"Work in progress, but what about you?"

"Yes, same old."

"Interesting assignments?"

"Yes."

"What sort of things?"

"Dodgy politicians, dodgy businessmen, that sort of thing. Let's just say my inbox is full." She leant forward and touched his hand. "Are you ready for some work?"

"Yes, if I can help you."

She looked serious suddenly. "Well, I don't know, to be honest. We'll see. This might be a particularly sensitive one."

"Well, what am I doing here, if things are so sensitive?"

"Why not? You've signed the Official Secrets Act."

"True, but …"

"Don't argue, I need someone I can trust."

"Well, I can manage that," Jack admitted. "What's the job?"

"We are here to meet a political party worker. Phillip Allardyce is his name. He's one of the deputy chairmen of the party."

"Which party?"

"The government."

Jack groaned. "A politician. Good luck in getting the truth."

Amanda ignored this. "Apparently he's got something to tell us."

"Why out here?"

"Oh, I don't know. He's got a reputation as an anti-establishment type, so he probably doesn't want to be seen with shady organisations like MI5."

"What's he going to tell us?"

Amanda laughed and got up. She knelt near him and kissed him lightly on the cheek. "I've no idea. That's what we're going to find out. We're meeting him in about fifteen minutes. Time to get ready."

Jack tried for another kiss but she was out of reach. "My bag's down the stairs, I'll go and get it."

"Fine, here's the key for your room. It's next door."

Chapter 6

Jack and Amanda arrived in the restaurant on time. Annoyingly, there was no sign of the man Allardyce. Amanda sat silently and had volunteered no further information on their guest. Jack didn't need any more information and was already satisfied with his prejudged view of Allardyce. Not that Jack was political, certainly not with a capital P. These days his views couldn't be coded into a single political movement; he preferred an easier method of listing things he was against. This was a long list and included almost everything Allardyce's party stood for.

Amanda tapped his arm and Jack looked up and spied a man of middle age entering the restaurant. He was wearing a pair of dull brown corduroy trousers and a patterned sweater. The sweater was inadequate in every way. It looked terrible, was too short and could not even cover up the multi-coloured shirt and non-matching tie beneath. Inevitably, Allardyce sported a beard. Not one of those modern well-kept beards, but a stringy irregular mess straight out of the flower power age. Judging people on appearance was nearly always a mistake, but Jack had made up his mind as the perfectly formed political caricature advanced and sat down beside them without a word.

Jack studied him closely, wondering why Allardyce exhibited no sign of a lack of confidence. Just the opposite in fact. Allardyce looked firstly at Amanda and then at Jack with an expression of superiority and, possibly, contempt. He had the confidence not to open the conversation and mustered only a monosyllabic grunt and a glance at his watch when Amanda ventured, "Good evening, Mr Allardyce."

Amanda introduced Jack, then had another go at pleasantries. Allardyce turned down her offer of a drink, so she got down to business. "Okay, Mr Allardyce, you have something to discuss with us?"

Allardyce's face tightened, and he shook his head. The tone of his red-brick voice told of an unpleasant task grudgingly undertaken, and he started with a formal disclaimer. "I am here at the direction of my party chairman, Colin Patterson. He feels that this is something that should be looked into."

"Okay …" Amanda said.

"Firstly, can you tell me who you represent, Miss Barratt?"

"I report to the Home Office."

"Does this mean that the home secretary will be privy to our discussions?"

"Not necessarily. It's at my discretion."

"You have a lot of power, Miss Barratt. Who's your boss?"

"Nick Devoy."

"You report directly to him?"

"Yes."

Allardyce delved into his wallet, from which he produced a folded sheet of paper, which he placed on the table. Amanda picked it up, unfolded it and held it up so that both she and Jack could read it.

The epistle was certainly not a classic. It had no address, no signature and was constructed with little consideration to neither penmanship nor grammar. It didn't take long to digest.

It read simply,

"The prime minister's a hypocrite. Talks about family values, but it's all talk. I know about the lifes he's ruined and the affairs he's had – with men and women. Five thousand pounds or I go to the newspapers. I'll be in touch."

Jack shrugged. "Surely this belongs in the bin?"

Allardyce jumped in. "Yes, I tend to agree. I told the chairman that this letter's a load of nonsense and we should just ignore it. I can't think why Colin felt it necessary to consult you guys. So, your advice is to ignore it?" he said hopefully.

Amanda ignored this question. "This is a photocopy?"

"Yes, the original is with the chairman."

"Well, we'll have to see that."

"If there is anything to investigate," Allardyce retorted.

"When was it delivered?"

"Three, maybe four weeks ago."

"And to whom was it addressed?"

"The party chairman, Colin Patterson."

"A bit old fashioned, a letter?" Jack said.

Allardyce said, "Well at least it's less easily traced than an email."

"Who opened the letter?" Amanda asked.

"I open all the mail for the party chairman."

"Do you still have the envelope?"

Allardyce shook his head slowly. "Sorry. It didn't seem important."

"Well, after you read the note, didn't you look for the envelope?"

"No." He added by way of testy self-justification, "After I read the note, I went directly to see Colin Patterson. We discussed it and," he added indignantly, "he didn't say anything about the envelope to me."

Amanda said, "mmm", and it didn't sound like a compliment. It was true that in a minor affair such as this, it was pretty unlikely that the letter would have much significance, but bungling like this at the outset of any enquiry usually boded ill for the future.

"And did anyone see who delivered this note?" she asked.

"No, it was handed in at the reception and was put on a pile of letters."

"You didn't ask?"

"The reception was unmanned that day."

"Have you CCTV?"

Allardyce thought for a moment. "Some, but it's a bit old."

"Have you checked?"

"Not yet."

Amanda uttered another grunt of dissatisfaction, then, evidently bored with Allardyce's down-his-nose attitude and perfectly mirroring Jack's thoughts, said, "Let's cut the crap, Mr Allardyce. You don't want to be here, and we don't want to be here either. So, please just tell us what it is your boss wants us to do."

Allardyce took this attack surprisingly well and came to the point quickly. "The party chairman thinks that we ought to, er, sub-contract this problem. If indeed there is a problem. So, I'm instructed to request that" – he turned his eyes skyward as he said it – "the authorities look into the matter. Discreetly, of course. We cannot allow any of this to get in the public domain. Our political opponents must not learn of this. Your investigation will naturally involve referring back to myself as necessary," he concluded pompously.

Jack looked at Amanda. He had a good idea of what she was thinking, but her features remained neutral. Allardyce surely didn't imagine that it would be as easy as that?

"Well, we will of course be in touch should we require further information," Amanda said. "Has Mr Patterson any reason to believe that the suggestions in this note are accurate?"

Allardyce looked appalled. "No, of course not. The chairman is only concerned about misinformation circulating. Also that this is a blackmail attempt, and the chairman thinks that it should be shut down."

"Does the prime minister know about this note?"

"He can hardly be troubled with this sort of nonsense."

"Anyone else?"

"Not that I know of. I opened the envelope, went to the chairman, and that's it."

"And you think the note is nonsense?" she asked.

"Yes."

"Is there anything else that might be relevant to my enquiries?"

Allardyce was irritated now. "No, Miss Barratt. We don't keep dossiers on people, not like your organisation."

Amanda laughed mirthlessly. She lifted the note and placed it in front of her. After studying it again for a second or two she folded it, and said, "Fine. Well, Mr Allardyce, that is quite clear. Now, will you dine with us?"

Jack was horrified as he detected a faint softening in Allardyce's features. He chipped in with an openly hostile stare at Allardyce. Then Allardyce looked at his watch again. Jack was relieved.

"No, thank you, I have a lot of important work to do. How long will it take for you to investigate this?"

"I can hardly say, Mr Allardyce."

Allardyce tried again. "The chairman asked me about that. What will I tell him?"

"Tell him we'll be in touch. Now if there's nothing else?"

"No, nothing. I expect you'll be in touch with any progress?"

Amanda flashed a smile of polite insincerity and Allardyce was gone.

Jack felt keenly that there was no time to lose in beginning a denunciation of Allardyce, but the man just wasn't worth it, so he accepted the menu she handed him.

"What do you want?" she said

"Oh, just a medium-rare steak."

She ordered two, put the miserable note in her bag and said, "What do you make of that?"

Jack laughed. "I can't stand Adam Chandler, but there's nothing in this, surely?"

"Probably not," Amanda agreed.

"What do you know about Chandler?"

"Working class boy made good. Scholarship to Oxford. Good on television and the public like him."

Jack wanted the salacious details. "What about his personal life? That's what this note's talking about."

Amanda shrugged. "Not much. Married for years, no kids. Nothing out of the ordinary as far as I know."

"There you are. A load of rubbish and no one gives a damn."

"Not quite true."

"What do you mean?"

"I mean someone gives a damn, and I can't think why."

"Like who?"

"Like Allardyce and Patterson."

Chapter 7

Jack hated hotels and he slept badly, so although it was barely six o'clock, the three loud thuds on his bedroom door hardly inconvenienced him. He threw on a robe and opened the door.

Amanda pushed past him and sat on the bed. "Get dressed."

He looked at her through heavy eyelids. She looked serious, so he decided not to argue and headed to the bathroom.

"I've just had a call, from my boss," she called.

Jack yawned. "Really?"

She said blandly, "Yes, about Allardyce."

Jack yawned again. "I don't want to speak to him again."

"Don't worry about that. You won't have to. He's dead."

"Eh? What happened? An accident?"

"I don't know anything yet. Hurry up."

Jack emerged from the bathroom, fastening his last shirt button, and followed Amanda who led him through a reception area and out the front door of the neo-Georgian hotel. She stopped and looked right and left.

"Are we taking one or both cars?" Jack asked.

"Neither."

She opted to go right and along a narrow-paved pathway that separated the hotel from a front lawn. At the gable end she turned right again.

Some hundred yards ahead, a group of men stood at the bottom of what looked like an external fire escape.

"Allardyce is here?" Jack said.

"Yes."

In a rude circle outside a closed white tent stood four men: two uniformed policemen and two in suits.

One of the men took a step towards them. He smiled at Amanda and ignored Jack.

Amanda smiled back. "Hello, Mike."

Mike slipped his hand into Amanda's and they engaged in a friendly, very friendly, welcoming embrace.

Amanda detached herself. "This is Jack, Jack Edwards."

Jack moved forward awkwardly and shook the man's hand. His rival was depressingly formidable and without any obvious flaw. He was taller than Jack, a little over six feet, and he was broader, not overly so but just enough to notice. He was about Jack's age but, on any measure, a lot more handsome. His hair was randomly distributed around his head but its overall effect, Jack was sure, would prove pleasing to women. Overall, the face represented a fine balance of cragginess and experience but with a strong enough hold on youth to be more than acceptably attractive. His greyish eyes were sharp and arresting, and, as if this was not enough, he had a definite look of intelligence.

All these fears seemed confirmed when he spoke. In an accent that would have served in any company, he said, with no suggestion that he felt or shared any of Jack's competitive spirit, "Nice to meet you, Jack," and added, covering for Amanda's omission, "I'm Chief Inspector Mike Richards."

He seemed to be a nice guy and Jack already disliked him.

The other men silently parted and withdrew a pace or two as Richards led Jack and Amanda into the temporary tent. Inside, a couple of men in white suits were working hard on items on a temporary and flimsy table. On the ground alongside there was a crumpled sheet.

"You finished with him?" Richards asked.

A voice came back. "Yes."

Richards bent down and pulled the sheet aside. Jack had seen a few dead bodies, but it was early in the morning. He hadn't bothered with a jacket and the cool of the morning was sharp. Maybe that was why he was shivering?

He hadn't exactly solved the case, but one look was enough to convince him that the fall had been a long one. The first rule of negotiating such a fall was to impact with one's feet with knees bent. The second was to have your hands over your head to protect it from the secondary impact when the body bounced. Allardyce evidently hadn't managed either of these things, and his head and neck were scrambled and fused into a sickening unidentifiable mash.

Amanda and Richards had strong stomachs and were kneeling over the body, talking in low voices. Jack had seen more than enough and he took a step back, opened the tent flap and sucked in fresher air and the welcome light rain which was now falling.

He walked towards the cold black iron fire escape and then looked up. The building was only four storeys high but it was a high-ceilinged Georgian design, and the roof, where the staircase seemed to start, looked about a hundred feet above. Amanda emerged from the tent and came across. She touched him affectionately on the arm. "Are you okay?"

"It's not much of a start to the day."

"No," she agreed.

Jack looked up. "Did he fall from these stairs?"

"No, not the stairs."

"Why not?"

She pointed upwards. "Each section is completely contained. I mean, someone could fall down some steps, but not out, not onto the ground below."

He looked up and that seemed to be true. "So, he fell off the roof?"

"Yes, probably. That's what Mike thinks."

"What was he doing on the roof?"

"There's an unofficial smoking area up there. There's a door that leads to it just off his bedroom."

"Allardyce didn't look like a smoker to me."

"What does a smoker look like?"

"I don't know, but he didn't seem the type to me."

"Maybe not, but it seems that he must have been up there. He had a cigarette stuck fast to the sole of his shoe, and he didn't get that from the fall."

Jack shivered again with thoughts of the sickening impact.

Amanda said, "Come on, let's get you a coat and we'll have a look up there."

He picked up a coat from his room and, now dressed like a detective, followed Amanda to the top floor of the hotel. At the end of a bland corridor there was a policeman standing outside a room which Jack supposed had been tenanted by the late Allardyce.

Amanda flashed him a warrant card. "Where's the door to the roof?"

"That way, ma'am. Last door."

After a short walk along another corridor, the way to the fire exit was clearly marked. Up a short double flight of stairs a heavy fire door was negotiated, and they emerged onto a section of flat roof that abutted the main pitched slate section. On a different day, Jack might have remarked upon, and even enjoyed, the extensive views, but he had his head down, giving exaggerated care to every step.

The felt roofing area was solid underfoot. It was covered by grit and dust carried by the wind and surrounded by a low sandstone wall about two feet high, broken only by the heavy gate indicating the entrance to the fire escape. The door swung open with a light push. The immediate area was littered with cigarette ends and a lightly used standing ashtray. Ahead, the staircase was taped off.

Amanda said, "They have done a first sweep of the staircase. Nothing there. Judging from the position of the body, he probably fell off the roof over there."

She led him to the roof edge and casually put a foot on the low wall while Jack kept a pace back. She looked over the edge. "Long way down."

"I'll take your word for it."

She then conducted a slow sweep round the roof but discovered nothing. "Come on, let's see his room."

The policeman moved aside and opened the door.

Richards stood framed by the bathroom door.

"Anything?" Amanda asked.

Richards shook his head. He moved and pointed to a small bag. "Just a few essentials in that. He was only booked in for one night."

All three conducted a short silent review of the room, which yielded nothing.

Jack said, "Doesn't smell like a smoker's room. I suppose there are no cigarettes here?"

"No, nothing."

"Matches, lighter?"

"No."

"Did you find either on or near the body?"

"No."

Jack was pleased with his contribution. He knew smoking knowledge would prove useful one day. He looked at Amanda, who allowed herself a grudging nod. "No sign of any struggles here?"

Mike said, "The room is completely clean."

"What about staff?"

"Nothing. We've spoken to all of the staff and checked them out. They're all local. Hard to believe any of them are hiding anything. Allardyce has no connections around here as far as we know."

"CCTV?" Amanda asked.

Richards shook his head. "Nope." He handed her a sheet of paper. "That's the guest list."

Jack looked over Amanda's shoulder. There were about a dozen names, including his and Amanda's.

Amanda said, "Have you spoken to all of them?"

"Yes, I'll get the notes to you, but nothing amiss. A few salesmen, a couple of holidaymakers, but I've kept them all here meantime. I'm not really sure what I should be looking for. I wanted to speak to you first. What were you guys talking to him about last night?"

Amanda lied smoothly, "Oh, routine. Allardyce was a deputy chairman of our governing party. He worked with Colin Patterson, the party chairman."

Richards said, "Yes, he was carrying a party membership card. Sorry, we phoned Patterson. I didn't know you were here."

"What did he say?"

"Not much. He took it calmly enough and seemed more bemused than shocked. Typical politician – it only took him about three sentences before he started on the need for keeping things low key and worrying about political damage. He pressed me a bit on what had happened, but I said we didn't know much and would see him later." Richards reflected, "So much for political friendships. Patterson actually said that Allardyce was pretty insignificant in the party. Not much of an obituary. Anyway, he's expecting us later. Should we go ahead?"

"Yes, just proceed as normal. So, unofficially where are you at?"

Richards shrugged. "Accident, maybe a suicide. Nothing else I can see." He narrowed his eyes a little. "Unless you can suggest anything else. After all, you guys might have been the last to see him alive."

Jack was sure that Richards would be interested to learn about the purpose and details of last night's meeting, but Amanda was keeping that to herself. The thought that he knew something the perfect Richards did not was a good one.

"No, nothing, but I'll call you later after you've talked to relatives."

Richards said, "As far as I know, there are no relatives, at least according to Patterson."

"I'll catch up with you later." Amanda turned to Jack and said, "Let's go."

He turned on his heel, pleased to get out of the room. For a split second, though, she wasn't alongside, and he turned and again became unreasonably irritated when he looked back and observed her in an au revoir clinch with Richards.

She caught up with him and playfully linked her arm in his.

"Old friend?" Jack asked.

"Yes, we were at Hendon together for a year."

"And you've kept up, I see."

She leant forward and, smiling, looked at him. "Are you jealous?"

He shook his head. "Don't be silly."

Chapter 8

Colin Patterson blew hard and struggled for breath. Only three steps to go, but that was still tough for a short man pushing sixteen stone. Back in his office, he fell heavily into the soft sofa.

Patterson was a working-class man of about sixty who, thanks to his parents' zealous enthusiasm for education, had made what most would describe as a success of his life. His political rise had been traditional. A union official slowly rising up the ranks and gradually becoming more prominent in matters political until, upon the death of a long-standing Member of Parliament, he was selected for an easily winnable parliamentary seat, which he represented to this day.

His time in Westminster had gone well. Powerful oratory had given him early prominence, then his keen grasp of detail and ability to bully the weak and fawn to the strong had allowed him to advance rapidly. He had enjoyed spells both in and out of government, mostly in senior positions. And then the prime minister had unexpectedly retired. Patterson was well-placed and had a lot of backers. An easy run-off against a lightweight candidate. But the lightweight candidate had done very well in the first round, tying his vote. Then all his so-called friends had jumped ship. Apparently it was time to skip a generation, and Adam Chandler sailed to the premiership.

At the time, Patterson put a brave face on it, expecting that he would be rewarded with a senior position, but Adam Chandler was a new broom, a modern politician, and had no place for Patterson and his out-of-date attitudes and connections. As a sop, he had been offered the party chairmanship – in political terms a calculated, public humiliation.

Patterson's first instinct had been to turn this offer down, but eventually he had accepted it, arguing that it would keep him in touch with the party organisers and distance him from government's failures. And there would be many failures. In the meantime, as he had nothing to do, Patterson had been happy to accept his ministerial salary, be driven in his Jaguar and wait. The workload was light, save for occasional attendance at unimportant meetings. His staff numbered about twenty, who, at least in name, could be directed to his whim, but that was never true in politics. Patterson couldn't trust any of them.

He poured a large brandy and scanned the office for the box of cigars.

He enjoyed his office. When you'd been one of eight, raised in a two-up, two-down terraced house, you spent the whole of the rest of your life yearning for space and privacy. Patterson had hit the jackpot. It wasn't one of those modern ergonomically perfect offices, just an over-the-top old-fashioned version about as big as a football pitch.

The leather-topped antique oak desk, supported by four elephantine legs, contained a single report only. A low priority review of party fundraising. It needed a detailed, line-by-line assessment, but he would probably just write "no comments" and file it somewhere in the north-east portion of the office. The report could wait.

He headed past the meeting table into a further area, which was devoted to chairs and a sofa and was dominated by a large wall-mounted television. Alongside was an oak sideboard, home to a variety of modern, and mostly unused, modern communications paraphernalia. He ignored that as well and continued to the well-stocked liquor cabinet.

Now he had a tougher decision. The twelve-year-old malts looked good, but he settled for brandy.

He poured a double, maybe a triple, and headed back to the sofa, which he fell into lazily and, after a moment, turned on the television and began to watch nothing in particular.

After a spot of channel hopping, he gave up on that and, with difficulty, pushed himself off the sofa. He poured another. It was time for a little exercise, so he headed across the office and out the French doors, which led to a good-sized balcony. Below, the throngs of people busied themselves with whatever the little people did. Far below, he watched the moving figures, watching how the other half lived. Unlike most of them, he had a tough job, but Patterson knew that someone had to do it and, if it took self-sacrifice from someone at the top, well, he was your man.

He withdrew back into his office and spared a thought for his dead deputy. They had been colleagues for about a decade but he really knew nothing about him. He supposed that he could have found out more, but he really hadn't been interested. Allardyce was just not an interesting man. The only thing that was interesting was the way he had died. Patterson supposed it must have been an accident. He certainly hadn't marked Allardyce down as a suicide. Always dedicated to the party and his cause. His childish cause. A man that believed he could actually change anything, all wrapped up in theoretical Utopian drivel.

Patterson was forced to admit that he hated Allardyce, but given the feeling was mutual, he didn't feel so bad about it. He was gone now and who really cared?

There was only one thing they had agreed upon: their hatred of Chandler. Both of them knew that Chandler was a fraud and that he couldn't last.

And then Chandler had won the general election. Easily.

Patterson had fallen out of love with the public at that point. Why couldn't they see what he could see? He had no answer to that, so he had given up, out of energy and ready to coast to retirement. That wouldn't be so bad. And then things changed.

He and Alexis had never been the romance of the century, but that was nothing to do with Chandler, and it was surprising how much it hurt. Maybe, under other circumstances, he would have just let things take their course, but now it seemed different. Chandler had taken almost everything from him. He was a man. He had to do something.

The only good news was that there was something that he could do. They said that Chandler had quite a few skeletons in his cupboard. He hadn't really believed it, but true, or otherwise, Patterson had found a new mission and now was devoted to chasing down every rumour. He still had contacts in the media, and recent conversations had been promising.

For most of his life, Patterson had envisaged a productive life, with a superficial devotion to so-called public service, but that had long gone, replaced by a bleak nothingness in which, whatever else happened, Chandler must be destroyed.

Chapter 9

As usual Amanda did the talking and, with Jack a pace behind, they were admitted to the office of Colin Patterson.

"Homely," Jack observed.

Amanda smiled, and they waited as Patterson walked across from the balcony and indicated seats.

Amanda introduced them both.

"Home Office?"

Amanda said, "You will get a visit from the police, Mr Patterson, but in certain sensitive cases, the Home Office takes an interest – besides which, we met with Mr Allardyce last evening, at, I understand, your direction."

Patterson took a mouthful of brandy.

Jack didn't want a drink, but it would have been nice to be asked.

"The police will update you on Mr Allardyce's death. Mostly, I'm interested in the note, the blackmail note, which we talked to Mr Allardyce about last night."

Patterson said airily, "Yes, yes of course. I wasn't sure of the time of your meeting. The police didn't mention that. They said that Phillip had fallen from a roof, and they would update me later."

Amanda said, "Yes. Anyway, we met with him last night."

Patterson said vaguely, "Really it seems extraordinary."

"Why extraordinary?"

"Well, I don't know the details. It's just a shock."

"Was he a suicide risk?"

"No, of course not. The police on the telephone said it was an accident."

"Well, they have not yet come to a final decision. Nothing is ruled out, although leaping from a building is not a common suicide method. Tell me about him."

"There's very little to tell. Phillip has been a party worker for years. He really didn't have any other interests, as far as I know. He is, I mean was, very committed and very energetic for the things he believed in. You met him last night. Did he seem strange?"

Amanda shrugged. "Normal enough."

Everything about Allardyce had been strange as far as Jack was concerned, but he said nothing.

Patterson said, "But how much do we ever know about people?"

Amanda ignored this philosophical question. "Was he working on anything unusual?"

"No, nothing in particular."

"Other than this blackmail note."

"Yes, but I can't see what that's got to do with it. We get things like this so often."

"So, I understand. Yet you wanted us to investigate?"

"We must always do our best to avoid scandal."

Amanda said, "Can I see the original of the note? Mr Allardyce only had a copy."

Patterson said, "Sorry, I had a look for it, but it seems to have been mislaid."

"Please have another look. I want to see it."

"I'll try, but it was an ordinary single sheet of paper."

Jack, growing tired of the slow pace of the discussion, said, "But what made you think that this note, out of the dozens you receive, was any more important than others?"

Patterson turned his head upwards. "No particular reason, to be honest. I suppose the note was a bit more specific than most." He shook his head. "But other than that, I don't really know. Sometimes you just get a nose for these things."

Amanda said, "When was this note delivered?"

"Three, maybe four weeks ago."

"Why didn't you act immediately?"

"At first, it seemed unimportant."

"And why's it important now?"

Patterson said, "Nothing's really changed. It just didn't seem urgent, but after a little reflection it seemed prudent to investigate. Three weeks or so to make a decision on something is not that long."

"Have you any idea who sent the note?"

Patterson narrowed his eyes. "Of course not."

"And who else knows about it?"

"No one, of course. It's not the sort of thing one publicises."

"Yet you decided to contact us?" Amanda said.

"I'm sure I can count on your discretion, Miss Barratt."

"How well did you know Mr Allardyce?"

"I have known him for about ten years, but it's only in the last year or so that I've known him better as a colleague."

"Was he ever a Member of Parliament?"

"No, he preferred working in the party."

"Why?"

Patterson shook his head slightly. "Phillip was always reluctant to compromise on his beliefs. He saw his role as being an activist within the party."

"To promote policies sometimes at odds with the government line?"

"Quite often," Patterson admitted.

"Did you appoint him?"

Patterson shook his head. "No, that was a prime ministerial appointment also. It was made at the same time as I was appointed chairman."

"I understand that he was a political opponent of the prime minister?"

Patterson shrugged. "We're a broad church. Why upset a wing of the party?"

"And you liked him?"

"He was efficient and committed to our success."

It didn't sound much of an endorsement to Jack. "Did you see eye to eye? On policy, I mean?"

"Well, there are always little differences, even between colleagues, but we were also absolutely committed to the same ends. Inevitably there are day-to-day disagreements about how we get there." He added, insincerely, "He will be missed."

Amanda said, "Mr Allardyce seemed unconvinced on the importance of this note."

"Of course. I'm sure that there's nothing in it."

"Yes, but I got the impression that he would rather not have spoken to us?"

"Phillip was not always comfortable with the forces of authority."

Amanda smiled humourlessly. "So, there's nothing else you can tell me?"

"No, nothing, I think."

"Oh, last thing, Mr Patterson. Was Mr Allardyce a smoker?"

"Oh no, he hated it."

Amanda stood up, and Jack did the same. She moved to the door without shaking Patterson's hand. "Thanks for your time, Mr Patterson. As for Mr Allardyce, the police will be in touch." She halted at the open door. "I'm going to need the original note."

"I'll try."

"Try hard, Mr Patterson. I intend to follow this up."

Chapter 10

It was surprisingly easy to visit the headquarters of a political party after business hours. Alarm coverage was patchy and security was feeble. Some of the lifts had cameras, the main stairs a few, but there were none here.

Not far now. A right-hand turn into a short corridor ended abruptly with a single door, wooden and heavy. Its bold brass plate told that it was the right door. An ear pressed against the door detected the sound of a television. And then a speculative look through the keyhole. Clear.

The large brass handle turned easily and noiselessly. The door was equally co-operative and made no audible demur when slowly pushed forward. The television blared on, but there were no other sounds inside. A large, cavernous room, full of good furniture but empty of people.

An experienced scan revealed only one issue. A door beside the desk was a potential problem. Light powerful steps. The door was locked. Good.

Behind the large antique desk, a fine white-lace curtain danced inside a gap between two French windows. Traffic sounds came from outside.

The man was looking out from the balcony. Thick plumes of cigar smoke surrounded him. He was holding a drink and he took a mouthful. He turned, maybe to pour another, but he would never have another. The way was barred. The man opened his mouth but made no sound. He tried a quizzical glance, but it wasn't answered.

Youth, strength and clarity of purpose were always going to prevail. A hundred feet was quite high, but it only took a few seconds for the body to reach the pavement below.

The sound of the London traffic droned on, unaware of, and indifferent to, the fact that Colin Patterson's political career was over.

Chapter 11

By Jack's calculation, Colin Patterson had fallen from about the same height as Phillip Allardyce, but his descent had caused a lot more inconvenience. Closing a key road in central London generated a lot more news coverage than inconveniencing residents at a car park in an Essex hotel. It was probably a status thing. Patterson would have approved.

Jack watched from the pavement as Amanda and a throng of suited people surrounded another depressing white tent in the middle of the road. Mostly there was no civilian traffic, except for a couple of saloon cars, one with a deep depression on its long bonnet, possibly caused by the flying chairman.

Amanda walked across. "Sorry, this is taking a while."

"Patterson is an important man."

"Not that important now."

"Harsh."

"Sorry."

"Another accident?"

"Well, I haven't got any other evidence, except that I don't believe in coincidences."

"Neither do I," Jack said, "but what else is there?"

"Come on, let's have a look inside the building."

They passed a solitary policeman at the entrance and walked into the reception, which was manned by a long-haired youngster who

Jack recognised as Max Harris, a technical protégé from Amanda's department.

"You remember Max?"

"Yes."

Max muttered an acknowledgement but didn't look up, preferring to concentrate on a row of old-fashioned screens and uttering a series of tuts.

Amanda said, "Have you got anything?"

"Nothing. This CCTV is rubbish. It only covers the reception area and the first floor, and there's nothing to see there."

"Surely they cover the fifth floor? That's where all the senior folks are."

"No. They moved from the first-floor last year but didn't update the system."

"What about the lifts?" Amanda asked hopefully.

"Sorry."

"Who's here after five?"

"One security guard. He spends some time at this reception but seems to prefer a little office down the corridor."

"Have you spoken to him?"

"Briefly. He's still here."

It wasn't exactly a broom cupboard but it had brooms in it. It also had a small dangerous-looking gas cooker, which was working hard, urging a large, battered iron kettle to the boil.

Sergeant Cook's uniform was dull and well-used but it fitted him well for a man of about sixty. He had lost none of his military manners and he stood up tall, just stopping short of a salute, when Amanda led Jack inside.

She sat down on the only other seat in the room, reached across and removed a cigarette from a packet.

Cook sat down. "Hello, ma'am."

"Hello, John. How are you?"

A few cardboard boxes served as a seat for Jack.

"Cup of tea, ma'am?"

"Yes, please."

Cook poured tea. He didn't acknowledge Jack but slapped a mug of black tea in his hand. He then reached for a small booklet, which he consulted carefully. "Arrived at 4.54. At reception until 6. Rounds 6 to 6.30. Checked staff book. Only the chairman still in the building. Rounds on the hour every hour until 8.54."

Sergeant Cook shut his book and trusted his memory. "I answered the door bell and spoke to PC Wilson, number 2462, an old Westminster Central number."

"What did he say?"

"That a man had fallen onto the road. That the area was cordoned off and could I account for everyone in the building. I rang up to Mr Patterson. There was no answer, so I went up to his office. No one there."

Amanda stood up. "Let's have a look."

Cook led them out of his office. After a claustrophobic lift journey, they arrived at the management floor.

A few scenes of crime officers were working on Patterson's office door. Amanda didn't go into Patterson's office but stopped outside. "Where does that door lead to, John?"

"Fire escape, ma'am."

She turned and beckoned a SOCO over, then pushed open the door, which revealed a broad concrete stairwell. She looked around for a moment and then began to descend. A few steps down she turned. "Come on."

Jack's heart sank – five floors. He was exhausted already.

At the bottom, nothing, and the push bar door looked blemish free.

"Is this alarmed, John?"

"No, I don't think so."

"Cameras?"

"No."

"How often are the fire drills?"

"Irregular, I'm afraid. I can check. There is a register that they keep at reception."

She turned to the SOCO. "Have you done this area?"

"No, ma'am."

"I want it done. Prints on this door or opening bar. Prints on the handrail. Everything."

"I'll need to call a team back."

"Yes, do it. Can we open the door?"

The SOCO did so and everyone emerged into a traditional cobbled alleyway, home to a few overflowing rubbish bins and not much else.

"Not many street lamps," Jack contributed, as he paced around the alley, looking at the ground for nothing in particular.

"Good work, Sherlock," Amanda said. "Now let's get back to the office."

After a tiring five-floor return, they returned to the office. Amanda moved across the room and straight to the balcony. "Were the balcony doors open when you came up?"

"Yes, ma'am."

They drifted out to the balcony, a sturdy stone-built promontory, guarded by curvaceous stone spars about five feet high. It was quite a spot, allowing a vista over the small, centralised power hub of the UK. With a large brandy in hand, it was probably tough not to feel superior.

Amanda said, "Did you go out to the balcony, John?"

"Yes, I had a quick look but there was nothing. I didn't look over the balcony. Why would I?"

"Why indeed?"

She turned to Jack. "Hard to fall over, if you ask me."

"He could have climbed?"

"Doubtful, Patterson looked out of shape to me."

"Maybe he stood on something?"

"Well, where is it then?" Amanda replied reasonably.

"There was nothing here when I came up," Cook said.

Jack said, "Do you think someone came up that fire escape?"

"Why not?" Amanda replied. "A clandestine assignment. What about that, John?"

"Not impossible, I suppose."

"Now, who would the chairman be letting in the back door after hours?"

Jack said, "A mistress?"

"Maybe. John?"

"Not to my knowledge. He often stayed late but always alone, drinking brandy. He drank a lot of that."

Chapter 12

Amanda knocked on a large black door. Someone opened it and she went through with Jack behind. Getting into No 10 Downing Street was easy.

They introduced themselves to a secretary who, in turn, led them through to a small uninhabited office, at the end of which stood a door. She knocked. "Excuse me, Miss Cahill," the public servant intoned, "Miss Barratt has arrived."

Cahill did not rise from her seat to greet them but, with a regal gesture, indicated chairs. The guests sat down and Cahill, still silent, undertook a careful, undisguised appraisal of them. She said, "Miss Barratt and …"

"Jack Edwards, attached to the Home Office," Amanda replied.

Cahill nodded and looked at Amanda. "I enjoy the full confidence of the prime minister in this matter and he has requested that I liaise with you and keep him fully informed on these appalling events. Obviously we will speak to Nick Devoy also."

Amanda said, "I have his full confidence and will liaise with you, and of course the prime minister if necessary."

Cahill narrowed her eyes, then allowed herself a thin smile. "Very well, Miss Barratt. I'm listening."

"Thus far we have no evidence of a state attack or co-ordinated domestic terrorism. These possibilities cannot be ruled out yet, but they represent a low probability at this time."

"And this leaves us with?"

"Accident, suicide … maybe old-fashioned murder."

"Which are you leaning towards, Miss Barratt?"

"None of the above at this stage."

"Could we not provisionally stretch towards 'tragic accidents'. The press should be told something. That would help to quell any irresponsible speculations. Besides, it's surely the most likely explanation."

"I can only tell you what we know as fact at the moment."

"Of course, but would you object to us briefing that we believe these are likely to be tragic accidents?"

Amanda said, "You must say what you wish, Miss Cahill. However, I have no particular objection, if it shuts up the media, although I doubt that it will."

"In that case, I'll issue something this morning. You will, of course, update us. When will that be?"

"Whenever I have news."

Cahill pushed her seat back. "Then our business is complete?"

"Just another moment, Miss Cahill. Are you aware of a note which was received at party headquarters a few weeks ago?"

"Note? What note?"

"A short and crude note." Amanda dipped into her pocket and dropped the copy on Cahill's desk.

"Is this a joke?"

"Mr Allardyce and Mr Patterson didn't think so. They asked me to investigate."

"How did they come to have this?"

"I understand it was delivered to party headquarters."

"When?"

"Several weeks ago. Did you not know about this?"

"No."

"Should you have been made aware?"

"Normally I would expect to be made aware of anything concerning the prime minister, although perhaps not with something so trivial."

Amanda said, "Not trivial according to Allardyce and Patterson."

"Well, their judgement was not always sound."

"Are you saying that you wouldn't have involved us?"

"Let's just say that these sort of crazy letters and emails are ten a penny in politics."

Amanda repeated, "Yet Colin Patterson and Phillip Allardyce took a different line and didn't inform you."

"I expect that they would have. I am rarely at party headquarters these days."

"When was the last time?"

"Last month, if that is relevant."

"Who can tell?" Amanda mused.

Cahill said, "Quite clearly this nonsense has no bearing on these tragic events."

"You will understand that we have to look at everything. It seems unusual to me for two senior members of your government to meet similar ends only a day or so apart."

"Hardly senior. Phillip Allardyce was, to be honest, a fairly minor party official."

"Colin Patterson was your party chairman."

"Well of course, but that's more of an honorary title. In reality he had little influence. But as you say, Miss Barratt, let's wait for the police. We must keep in mind the feelings of Colin's family."

"Yes of course. What about Mr Allardyce's family?"

"Oh, I understood he had no relatives, but to be honest, I didn't know him that well. I was thinking more of Alexis."

"Colin Patterson's wife?"

"Yes."

"Is she a friend of yours?"

"Not really. I mean, I know her. She writes a column in one of the Sunday papers."

Amanda returned to her favourite subject. "Mr Patterson told me that only he and Mr Allardyce knew about this note."

Cahill glanced at her phone and then a document in front of her. "If he said so, then presumably that was the case."

"Did the prime minister know?

Cahill looked up. "Hardly."

"Should I have a word with him?"

"Is that really necessary?"

"Probably not. For now."

"Good, you can be assured that I will keep the prime minster in the loop." Cahill leant over and handed the note back to Amanda.

Jack had enjoyed this exchange. If Amanda and Cahill had been speaking at a conference, both would have been proclaiming the imperative for more women in power. But there was no sisterhood bond here.

Amanda opened her mouth to speak, probably to irritate Cahill again, but she was interrupted by the opening of a connecting door.

Adam Chandler, the prime minister of Great Britain and Northern Ireland, appeared. He looked across at the visitors and then to Cahill before settling himself casually on the end of her desk.

Power was a funny thing. It demanded attention, and Jack found it hard not to stare at the leader of the nation. Not that he was much to look at. He looked a little older, a little shorter, and a lot balder than he did on the television.

After an introduction and some routine handshaking, Chandler said, "I understand that you are investigating the deaths of my colleagues, Mr Allardyce and our chairman, Colin Patterson."

"Yes."

"A great loss, both of them," he intoned blandly.

Amanda, apparently not awed by power, said provocatively, "Miss Cahill was telling me that their respective roles were no longer of great importance to the government."

Chandler narrowed his eyes. "We have modernised, yes. Colin was seen as one of the old guards, but I still valued his advice."

"Have you seen him recently?"

"Not for a couple of months."

"And he was fine then?"

"Completely normal as far as I'm concerned."

"And Phillip Allardyce?"

"Ah, Phillip, always a challenge. He never really saw eye to eye with me politically. Rather an idealogue, I'm afraid. Anyway, I wish you very well with your enquiries." He looked at Cahill. "I'll catch up with you later."

Amanda handed him the note.

Jack tensed and Cahill scowled.

Chandler read the note and, without comment, handed it back to Amanda.

"Did Mr Patterson talk to you about this?" she asked.

Chandler laughed. "Is this a joke?"

"Just one of these tiresome things. It was delivered to Colin Patterson anonymously a few weeks ago. He asked me to look into it."

Chandler said, "He didn't mention it."

"Why would he?"

Chandler held onto his agreeable smile. "Why, indeed. It's the sort of rubbish one has to listen to every day in this business."

"So Miss Cahill tells me."

"Quite so. Anyway, the priority is Colin and Phillip at this stage. If there is any way I can be of further help, let me or Sheila know."

"Thank you, prime minister."

He turned to leave, and Jack had a last look. Up close, an unremarkable man, and Jack wondered how it was that he had become prime minister. He was glad he hadn't voted for him.

Amanda nodded to Sheila Cahill, but Cahill's features were frozen hard with an expression that could only be described as hostile. Maybe she returned Amanda's valedictory nod, maybe not, Jack couldn't tell. All he did know was that she had not enjoyed meeting Amanda.

Chapter 13

After the meeting at Downing Street, Jack and Amanda strolled down Whitehall, enjoying the heat of the day.

"Well, what do you make of that?" Amanda said.

"Disturbing," Jack said.

"Chandler?"

"No, Cahill. Well, both of them really. It's worrying when you see, close up, the folks that run the country."

"They're just like you and me."

"Christ, I hope not, but that was all a bit edgy."

"What do you mean?"

"You and Cahill."

Amanda smiled.

"You made it obvious that you didn't like her."

"Not true."

Jack laughed. "This is me, just admit it."

"I would admit it if it was true. Look, Cahill's a master of spin, always on message. I wasn't interested in her messages, so why not mix things up a bit? See what happens."

"Just a tactic?"

"Yes, what does Cahill enjoy?"

"Power, I would say?" Jack ventured.

"A good answer. So, I remind her of the limits of her power. She doesn't like it, and we find out things about her."

"Maybe she's got more power than you?"

This time Amanda laughed out loud. "Perhaps, if you mean personally, but if you think that a here today, gone tomorrow politician has more power than the permanent civil service and security services, you have a lot to learn."

Jack said, "That's a vaguely depressing statement."

"Yes," Amanda agreed, while looking right and left at the blur of London traffic before hailing a black cab, into which she ushered him. "Apsley Street, Muswell Hill," she ordered the driver and then relapsed into the seat.

"Where now?"

"Off to see the grieving widow."

The taxi driver certainly had "the knowledge", and he used it to the limit with a succession of darting moves through the side streets of north London. Despite this, nose-to-tail traffic dictated that it took close on half an hour before the cab arrived in the tree-lined calm of Apsley Street.

"What number, miss?" asked the driver.

"Ten," Amanda said, and they continued down the road, passing substantial red-brick mansion houses set off from the main parade until the taxi pulled up.

Jack and Amanda walked up a short path and rang the doorbell. The door was opened by a tall woman, more than forty but under fifty, with ill-managed, shoulder-length, curly dark hair. On a good day she would have been good-looking, but that wasn't today. She looked at them with dead, black eyes.

Amanda said, "Mrs Patterson?"

The woman might not have been at her best, but she still had poise and, Jack thought, breeding. With a clipped accent, she replied, "Yes. What can I do for you?"

"We are here on official business about your late husband. Could we come inside?" She flashed an ID card at the woman.

"Come in, Miss Barratt."

They followed a few feet behind the woman as she led them through a spartan hallway and then through a door, which led into a large, well-furnished living room dominated by two expensive facing sofas.

There was a man in the room. Alexis Patterson sat closely alongside him and indicated the opposite sofa to her guests.

As they all tried to make themselves comfortable, Jack had a look at the man beside her.

His body was long and lean. His face was the same, lined and cragged with what looked like every one of life's vices etched upon it. His eyes were blue and maybe had once been piercing, but any sharpness and lustre had long since dulled. He glanced at Mrs Patterson. The man had to be her father.

Amanda reintroduced them both. "I am Amanda Barratt, Home Office, and this is Jack Edwards."

"Home Office?"

"Yes, we sometimes take an interest in certain high profile and sensitive public cases."

"I see." The woman indicated the man sitting alongside. "This is my father, Lord Hamilton." She volunteered no further information, but that wasn't necessary.

Jack knew him now. A well-known face in the British press. Quietly lauded by some, but nowadays more often loathed and ridiculed. Lord Hamilton came from one of the oldest aristocratic lines in England. Wealth, land and influence had been theirs for generations since the Norman Conquest.

With the Hamiltons it had been mostly influence, political influence and, although not so prominent as the Cecils or Norfolks, at most of the great events in English history there had been a Hamilton lurking somewhere. The present Lord Hamilton had followed firmly in the family tradition as a Member of the House of Lords, prominent in the governing party until one day, about ten years ago, when he had a brainstorm. After ten centuries of quiet manoeuvring, the current Lord, it seemed, could stand it no longer and had broken all conventional political ties. He had formed his own political party, Britain First. Jack knew nothing about its policies, just that the Guardian called them "extreme right wing".

He looked closely at Hamilton. How unprepossessing he seemed. Wasn't that always the way of potential dictators?

Amanda acknowledged Hamilton but didn't offer her hand. She said to Alexis Patterson, "Would you rather talk alone?"

Alexis Patterson tilted her head. "No, why would I?"

"As you wish."

Hamilton got into the action now. After downing a long mouthful of something from a large chunky tumbler, he said dismissively, "The police have already been here. I think we have told them all we can."

Amanda said. "Yes, I'm sure they have all the key details, but their enquiries tend to be a little narrower than mine." She turned to Alexis. "Your husband was an important figure. My job is to make sure there are no underlying public interest issues that are connected or, perhaps, unnecessarily become connected with the case."

Lord Hamilton chipped in. "Sweep stuff under the carpet, you mean?"

Amanda didn't answer that. "Just a few things, Mrs Patterson. Was your husband's mood as usual over the last week or so?"

"Quite normal."

"Any changes in routine?"

Alexis Patterson was expressionless and continued to present a dead bat. "No. Nothing different. My husband was a man of habit, Miss Barratt. He left the house at seven-thirty – a car took him to the office and he was there or hanging around Whitehall all day and often well into the night. He often came back late."

"Was his workload particularly heavy?"

"No, not really, but he enjoyed it."

"Did you ever see your husband during the day, Mrs Patterson?"

"Very rarely," she replied. "He had his work and I had mine."

Jack opened his mouth for the first time. "What work is that, Mrs Patterson?"

Alexis looked at him dismissively. "I write a weekly column in the Sunday Enquirer."

"What about?"

Her eyes narrowed and her voice delivered the full force of a paid-up member of the Hampstead set. "Political issues, mostly."

Jack knew all that but he said, "Oh."

Alexis went on. "I also do a lot with local charities, mostly working with the homeless. We have a local drop in-shelter."

Of course she did, thought Jack.

Amanda said, "And yesterday?"

She looked at Amanda without smiling and said testily, "I told the police about this already, Miss Barratt. I worked from home on my column, and after dinner I went to the shelter for a late shift."

"Did you take an interest in your husband's work, Mrs Patterson?"

"Not specifically, but my business is politics. However, I'm not really partisan, and my independence is crucial. Naturally, I went to a few functions and I sometimes scolded him about not doing enough for the homeless, but really" – and she glanced at her father – "there's quite enough party politics in the family."

"Did your husband have any enemies?"

"Political enemies, I suppose. Everyone has in politics, but not real enemies. Does this matter? Surely this was an accident?"

Amanda said airily, "It would be silly to rule anything out at this stage."

"Well, he didn't have enemies in the way you mean. Not people that would want to kill him. The idea's ridiculous."

"Were relations between you and your husband good?"

She looked hard at Amanda and Jack noticed a flash of colour in her weary features. She coldly replied, "As happy as the next couple."

"And how happy is that, Mrs Patterson?"

She laughed sadly. "Well, Miss Barratt, the next couple marry and spend a few years absorbed in each other and planning their lives together. Then the sex stops, and they realise that all they ever had in common was a short-lived mutual attraction. If they're lucky there are children, but, if not, then the next couple make the best of things."

It was a bleak analysis that Jack found hard to fault.

Amanda said, "Was your husband a heavy drinker?"

"Yes, pretty heavy. I mean, it goes with the job: receptions, long hours, Commons bars. But Colin," she added – it was the first time she had used his first name but it seemed for convenience rather than intimacy – "he was pretty used to it. I mean, he was very rarely drunk. Some people can take it and some" – here she looked at her red-eyed father – "cannot."

Amanda said, "So you'd be surprised to learn that your husband was drunk and stumbled over the balcony?"

"Do you believe that happened?"

Amanda shrugged. "It's a possibility."

Alexis said, "Accidents happen but yes, I would be surprised."

"So that leaves us with what?"

As Alexis Patterson considered these alternatives, her father made a gratuitous intervention. "Perhaps a sudden revelation of the futility of his political career overwhelmed him?"

Amanda said, "So you favour a suicide theory, Lord Hamilton?"

"Not favour, but it's a possibility."

"And you, Mrs Patterson?"

"I know of no reason why he would kill himself."

"And no reason why someone would have killed him?"

"Certainly not."

"What about you, Lord Hamilton? Can you add anything?"

The wrinkled peer clung tightly to his whisky tumbler and smiled at Amanda. "Are you not going to ask me about my work, Miss Barratt?"

Amanda smiled back. "Why waste time? I can read a file."

"Is it a large file?"

"Yes, quite large. Not a bad read."

"Glad you enjoyed it, Miss Barratt, and to answer your question, I know everything about my son-in-law's politics and I disapproved of them."

"What about Adam Chandler? Do you approve of him?"

"Not my kind of politician. A vacuous fraud."

"What about you, Mrs Patterson? Is the prime minister your kind of politician?"

Alexis got up and poured whisky for herself and another for her father. "Adam? Well, I voted for him, obviously, but I don't really know him all that well. As I've said, I'm not one for party politics really."

Lord Hamilton said, "And what about you, Miss Barratt?"

"Lowly public servants like me don't have opinions on these things," Amanda said.

Hamilton smiled at her. Evidently Amanda was his type of woman. "Not so lowly, Amanda. I've heard of you. I know Nick Devoy. He thinks very highly of you."

Amanda smiled back. "I didn't call round to discuss myself."

"That's a pity, but as for poor Colin, I know nothing that can help you, Miss Barratt."

"Where were you yesterday?"

Hamilton laughed. "In the house all day, working."

Amanda looked at Alexis Patterson. "Yes, I can confirm that."

Chapter 14

As they sat outside a Muswell Hill cafe, Amanda said, "What did you make of all that?"

Jack lit and then drew heavily on a cigarette and shrugged. "Not much. Alexis Patterson didn't seem to care all that much, and her father … well, I don't know how I would describe him."

Amanda smiled. "Surely you admired his plain speaking?"

"Not particularly. He liked you."

"Apparently he was a champion fornicator in his day."

"That sort never know when to quit."

Amanda pinched his arm and smiled. "There are others who never know when to start."

Jack laughed and said, "What else do you know about him?"

"Not much. He's really not taken very seriously, but it was better to puff him up a bit."

"I've now met Phillip Allardyce, Colin Patterson, Alexis Patterson, Lord Hamilton, Adam Chandler and Sheila Cahill. Quite honestly, I didn't like any of them. Selfish, out for themselves and worst of all, all useless. The funny thing is, I liked Hamilton best. He's nothing like they portray him in the newspapers, just a cranky old guy. The country's full of them."

Amanda laughed. "Almost no one in the public eye is as they're portrayed, surely you know that."

"Did you see how he looked at his daughter?"

"I didn't notice."

"No, but you were doing all the talking. I was watching him."

"And?"

"He adores her. Couldn't take his eyes from her."

"She's his only child. Seems natural enough."

"I suppose so. What now. Just wait on the police?"

"Let's have a coffee and think about this, especially what, if anything, this note has got to do with anything."

"Well, as to that note, you can forget it. It's the only thing I agree with Cahill on. This is the twenty-first century. No one cares about this sort of stuff nowadays. Patterson probably got drunk and fell off his balcony, although I must admit Allardyce beats me. I cannot think what he would be doing on that roof."

Amanda said, "Maybe both had meetings. Allardyce on the roof with someone who smoked and Patterson with someone he admitted via the fire escape after hours."

"I suppose that's possible, but you've got no evidence."

"None whatsoever," Amanda admitted.

"Let's suppose that this note is true for a moment, and further assume that some of the allegations are more politically damaging than just a few bedroom romps. If so, there must be a lot of people who would want this suppressed."

"Yes, but this works both ways. If these things are true there may be others who would want it to be investigated and to come out."

"Friends and enemies. Chandler will have plenty of both."

"I would think so."

"Maybe that's why Allardyce and Patterson were looking for an investigation, although Allardyce said he thought that the whole thing was nonsense."

Amanda said, "Yes, he said that, but do we believe him? He was a political opponent. I would have thought he would fit in the enemy camp."

"True enough. And Patterson?"

"I'm pretty sure he's not much of a Chandler fan, but I doubt he had the energy to do much plotting."

"But if they had a mutual dislike of Chandler, then why not these two being killed to stop something coming out?"

"Not impossible," Amanda said.

Jack drew on his cigarette. "Killed by a sitting prime minister: that would be a story."

"It would, but I think we can rule that out. It's rather easy to confirm a prime minister's movements."

"Have you done that?"

"I'm very thorough."

"So, you thought the prime minister might be involved. Incredible."

"Purely routine, don't get excited."

"Where does this take us?"

Amanda mused. "Chucking someone from a roof is a good assassination technique."

"Twice in two days?"

"Well, that's suspicious, but on the other hand, a couple of bullets in the head would make things completely clear."

"I suppose so, but the whole thing's too fantastic."

"Well, we don't have anything else at the moment. And two accidents or two suicides or two murders in two days is also fantastic as far as I'm concerned. Allardyce was an insignificant and fairly unimportant figure. We know that he had no connections with wilder political elements, and there's nothing in his background to even hint at the possibility of him having so formidable an enemy. But," she continued slowly, "he did know about that note. As for Patterson, he would have more enemies, but he also had little power. Why kill him?"

"Maybe the whole thing's nothing to do with politics. Allardyce, I can't say, but Patterson had a wife who didn't love him and his father-in-law probably hated him. Relations must have been strained. The deaths might be unconnected and have different causes."

Amanda sighed. "Yes that's possible, but two in two days."

"I know," Jack said.

Amanda sipped at her coffee and opened her mouth as if about to develop another theory but was interrupted by her mobile. After a short conversation she drained the last dregs of her coffee and said, "Time to go."

She hailed a taxi.

Jack said wearily, "Where to now?"

"Back to town. We've got our eyes on an individual. Apparently he turned up at the party headquarters and asked for Patterson."

"The author of that note?"

"Why not?"

"Obviously someone who doesn't read the newspapers. A real master criminal."

Outside Paddington railway station wasn't usually the best place to park a vehicle, unless you drove a black cab and could stop anywhere. Amanda handed the driver a twenty and didn't wait for change.

"Hurry up," she urged. A short dangerous sprint through unsympathetic traffic took them to the pavement near a street corner. Jack drew alongside her, breathing hard, but he wasn't allowed to rest and she took off again at something close to a jog.

Jack's lungs were bursting now. Old age and cigarettes. Something had to be done. Mercifully, she slowed, had a short discussion with a man in a suit, and changed to a slow walk. "There's our man."

Jack looked at a sea of people. "Which one?"

"The little guy, with the cheap sporty jacket. Do you see him?"

"No," Jack said. "Are you going to pick him up?"

"No, not yet."

They walked for some time, stopping occasionally in synch with their target. "Are special operations usually this boring?"

"Quite often. Just keep your eyes on our man."

"He's gone into that burger bar. Do we wait outside?"

"No, let's go in."

The burger bar was a relic from the seventies, having escaped the notice of the popular franchises. Two columns of plastic tables, some clean, about fifteen rows deep. They sat down at one of the many free tables and Jack reviewed the patrons. A bespectacled man of middle age suspiciously eyeing an unappetising thin-looking grey burger, a priest with a freely swinging crucifix. And finally, an adequately built middle-aged woman, tucking in with gusto into what looked, from the discarded wrappers, to be her fourth or fifth bun.

Their man stood waiting at a serving counter, covered by a single employee. He had shoulder-length, lank, dark hair and was dressed in trainers, a pair of jeans and a jacket modelled in the style of those worn by American football coaches.

The employee placed a tray with a smallish-looking order in front of the man. The man delved into his pocket and began carefully counting the coins that his hand had recovered from the depths. This exercise took a long time, but eventually the man lifted his tray, turned around and began to search for a vacant table. This easy task concluded, the man sat facing Jack and Amanda some six rows away and began to contemplate his meal. He was probably fifty, Jack thought, but he looked a lot older. His weight couldn't be more than eight stone and his grey, drawn jowls told of a man who had a very tenuous hold on this world.

Amanda sat in silence for a moment, then got up. Jack followed, and after a few steps they squeezed into a bench seat opposite the man.

"Hello, I'm Amanda, and this is my colleague, Jack."

"Colleague," the man repeated. "Are you police?"

Amanda didn't answer, but instead reached into her pocket and threw across the note. "Is this your work Mr …?"

"McMahon."

"Is it yours, Mr McMahon?"

McMahon looked at the epistle cautiously, then returned it to Amanda. In a soft Irish brogue, he said, "Not mine. My grammar is better than that."

"I understand that you have been looking for Colin Patterson?"

"I wanted to make a complaint about the government. I don't agree with their policies."

"Nor do I," Amanda admitted, "but complaining to Mr Patterson isn't going to help. He died yesterday."

"Oh."

"Don't you have a television or read the newspapers?"

"Neither."

"Very wise, Mr McMahon, but let's get back to this note." She turned the temperature way down on her voice. "Here's how this works, Mr McMahon. You can help me, and yourself, by telling me everything you know."

"How can I help myself?" McMahon enquired neutrally.

"Well, if all this amounts to is a note aimed at, shall we say, selling some information, and nothing to do with the deaths that I'm investigating, then ..."

"What deaths? I don't know what you're talking about."

"If that's true, then I can arrange for the matter of the note to be forgotten about."

McMahon looked at her shrewdly. "How do I know you have the power to deliver that promise?"

"Well, you don't. Basically, you can believe me or I can call the police and leave you to someone who doesn't have the power. There's a few of them outside. Shall I invite them in?"

McMahon looked at Jack, then back to Amanda.

"All right," he said. "What do you want to know?"

"Is this your note?"

"Yes." McMahon shook his head and admitted, "Pathetic, isn't it?"

"Did you really think that someone would pay?"

McMahon shrugged. "At the time I thought it was worth a shot, although I was drunk." From the smell of alcohol coming from McMahon, this explanation seemed plausible.

"What did you think you had on Adam Chandler?"

McMahon said, "Well, he is living a lie. He puts himself out there as a family man."

"Not much of a story these days," Jack contributed.

"Maybe not, but five grand's not a lot to him either. He's worth millions."

"Is he?" Amanda asked.

"Well, he must be," McMahon stated.

"How do you come to know things about Adam Chandler?"

"A friend of mine knew him well."

"Who?"

McMahon considered discretion but abandoned the idea. "Mikey Lynch, a friend of mine from Ireland."

"Address?" Amanda said hopefully.

McMahon looked at her closely and shook his head. "Sorry, he went home a year or two ago. He travels a bit and we've lost touch. I could see if I can find out."

"And how did Mr Lynch come to know things about the prime minister?"

"He worked as a porter at Oxford University for a year or so."

"Which college?"

"Merton, I think."

"Interesting. I was at Somerville."

Jack waited on Amanda to apply pressure, but she didn't. "All right, Mr McMahon, let me know about Mr Lynch. Oh, and your address?"

"Flat 48, Queens Road, Paddington. Do you know where that is?"

"Yes." She handed him a card. "And when you find Mr Lynch, you phone me, no one else. I'll expect to hear from you in a day or two, not longer. And Mr McMahon – no more notes." With this, she reached into her pocket and put a small collection of twenty-pound notes at the side of McMahon's plate. "There's more if you can help me quickly."

McMahon's eyes widened and he quickly pocketed the notes, muttering that he would do his best.

Once outside, a couple of suited men appeared alongside them, and Amanda muttered a few words to them.

Jack was getting the hang of this spy business. "Are you tailing him?"

"Let's say guarding him."

"On the basis that anyone who knows about that note is in danger?"

"I'm not sure."

"What about this Mikey Lynch character?"

"Adam Chandler was at Merton College. That much is true."

"And the rest?"

"I didn't believe it."

"Why didn't you challenge him?"

"Let's see what happens."

Jack said, "I think we could have got more out of him."

Amanda laughed. "Maybe I'll leave it to you next time. Come on – buy me a drink."

Chapter 15

When you were prime minister, life was more satisfying, stimulating and comfortable than that experienced by those one represented. The money was good, the expense account comprehensive and the lodgings were comfortable.

He'd wanted to be prime minister all his life and now he'd made it. Janice also liked the life. Their last wedding anniversary had been silver. There had been no children, and he couldn't remember whether there had ever been love. Either way, their political arrangement worked satisfactorily.

His job had only one minor drawback, and today Adam Chandler felt the unavailability of free time an oppressive restriction. It was about the only thing that hadn't occurred to him as he rose to the top, and although it might be a minor inconvenience, overall Chandler was listless, even bored. He needed more, he always needed more.

Today he would sate his boredom with the only thing he could think of to do. It wasn't much and it didn't really work these days, but in the absence of anything else he might as well go and see her. Maybe it would be better today? More likely it would be the last time.

It had all become too close and too intense and now, for Chandler, too risky. The last time they had met it had only been possible to break completely from prying eyes by being dropped off at her townhouse apartment. To achieve this, he had had to put himself in the power of an unknown government pool driver whom he had engaged after skipping out of a side door of 10 Downing Street. That might have to be done again.

At least today, Chandler had a bona fide excuse for contacting her. He pushed aside a sheaf of papers and picked up the phone.

Even a prime minister needed to be cautious on the telephone.

She answered after just two rings.

"Alexis, sorry to have taken so long to call you. I'm desperately sad about Colin and I just wanted you to know that he made a terrific contribution to the party and to public life and everyone, including me, is grateful and will miss him."

She replied formally. "Thank you, prime minister. I appreciate you finding the time to call."

"And you know, of course, that if there's anything you need, please don't hesitate to ask."

"Thank you, prime minister. There are many arrangements to make. I'm hoping for a meeting today, at 1pm, to make arrangements for the memorial service."

"Yes, of course."

Fifteen minutes later, Chandler, having, once again, been unable to think up a better subterfuge, slipped out of 10 Downing Street by the side door and sought out a car.

The driver accepted his commission readily. Whether he believed Chandler's claim of a headache and his request for a short drive was not certain. Chandler supposed that, of all servants of government, pool drivers had seen as much as most.

He had rehearsed this meeting for months. Probably she would be okay with it. She knew the score; she was from aristocratic stock, a class who understood that sexual appetites often had to be satisfied outside family units.

"Can you stop here, please? I want to visit an old friend."

"Yes sir," the driver said. He parked the Jaguar and pulled out a newspaper. "How long, sir?"

"I'll be about thirty minutes."

This proved to be fine with the driver, and Chandler strode rapidly along the street. He met no one, and from the garden path turned down a short flight of stairs and then through the unlocked basement door of the house.

At his arrival, she rose from the sofa and turned on her heel towards the bedroom. An advantage of having a mistress who was, or had been, married to a politician was that there was no need to explain the time and other pressures of the job. This, in turn, cut out any demand for insincere small talk or any other verbal foreplay.

There wasn't much time for any other foreplay either, but for him the sex was still okay, albeit routine: for her maybe a bit more, he wasn't sure. Not that he thought about that much. Was it five, maybe even seven years they had been meeting? He really couldn't remember.

"Alexis, wait a minute."

She turned and flashed him a puzzled look and returned slowly to the sofa.

He mixed himself a drink. "You want one?"

"No."

Chandler sat and opened with some time-honoured words. "Alexis, we need to talk."

"Do we, Adam?"

Chandler was one of the most articulate men in Britain. He was used to finding the right words in almost every situation, but he was struggling here. "Alexis, things are difficult at the minute. I mean, with Colin's death, the press is all over you. We need to be extra careful."

She lit another cigarette and settled a length of black hair behind an ear. "Of course, Adam, I understand that."

He looked at her. She was lightly but effectively made up and her ruby red lips were parted slightly. She stared back unblinking, nervous, almost childlike. He could almost remember why he had been attracted to her.

He juggled between getting straight to the business or softening the blow with some words about her late husband. He rejected the latter option and pressed ahead.

The childlike aspect to her features disappeared and she, not he, got straight to the heart of the matter. "Do you mean it's all over?"

The moment of truth.

"Well, cool it for a bit."

"How long did you have in mind, Adam? Ten years, twenty?"

He answered sharply, "Longer, if you like, Alexis."

"It's not that easy, Adam."

Of course it fucking is, he thought. "Come on, Alexis, we both know that we need to cool it. Just until things quieten down."

But she didn't know. "Why?" she demanded.

That was tough to answer, so he lit a cigarette instead.

"Do you like being prime minister, Adam?"

He shook his head. "Come on, Alexis."

"No, Adam, humour me. If you aren't going to fuck me, you can at least talk to me."

He leant towards her and extended his hand on top of hers. She threw it off violently. He sighed. "Yes, I like being prime minister."

"What about me, Adam? Do you like me?"

"Just stop it. Stop being silly. You know the answer to that."

"But Adam, you like being prime minister more?"

"Christ, this is getting us nowhere. I'm just suggesting we slow a bit, let things blow over."

"I know what you're suggesting, Adam." Not even a ticking clock broke the silence. "Don't flatter yourself that I need you. I don't – it's just that I choose to keep you."

"No, Alexis. It's over. We both need to move on. The press will be all over us with Colin's death."

She said menacingly, "Don't you dare mention Colin, you bastard. Now listen to me, Adam," and she added coldly, "and listen very well."

Chandler listened.

"You'll continue to meet me here as I require or else."

He checked his face as it started to fashion a sneer. He had spent years dealing with desperate people uttering threats with no cards to play. "Or else what, Alexis?"

"You'll find out. Come on."

He fashioned a resigned smile and followed her into the bedroom. Why not? He could dump her tomorrow.

Chapter 16

On the top floor of a three-storeyed town house, just off North Street in London, Bob Slater was already at work. A modest office. Slater hated wasting money.

He was forty-eight years old and was the kind of man that every man hoped to be at forty-eight: wealthy, healthy and powerful – he had everything under control.

He had founded, built up and sold many businesses, was on the board of many well-known companies across the globe, and his charitable activities were extensive. He was well-connected politically, having acquired friendships with politicians of all hues, mostly by the expedient of giving money to them all. He was a member of the MCC and all of the London clubs which he chose. He had never had time to marry or have children. He had been busy. It wasn't really a regret, and on Slater's vista no cloud interrupted the blue sky.

He picked up a bound document. Christ, it was heavy. Five hundred and fifty pages of a bland, uninspiring report from yet another committee formed to carry out yet another enquiry into transport links in the UK. Slater was the chairman of this committee, and he had hated every sitting.

His door opened. His assistant, Samantha. She anticipated everything. "Morning, Bob. What about the transport report?"

"I'll sit on it for two weeks, but the draft won't be changing. Lots of superficial nods to the green lobby – the words 'smart' and 'transformational' are everywhere."

"Do people really speak like that?"

"Just the experts that were on this committee, I think. No one else. Anyway, the big project goes ahead immediately, full funding over the next five years. Brief the usual people."

"Anything else?"

"Yes. I was able to rally them against the proposed new airport, so the landing slot prices will stay high for the foreseeable future. That's about it. What's in the diary tomorrow?"

"Nine o'clock working breakfast with the prime minister's task force on enterprise in inner cities, eleven o'clock board meeting of the Western Petroleum Group, twelve-thirty lunch at Simpsons with the minister."

"Okay, fine. I might go to Scotland for the weekend."

"And Sheila Cahill phoned. She asked for a meeting first thing."

"This morning?"

"She said it would be short and was urgent."

"Cahill?"

"She called last night. I told her to call back later, but she was pretty insistent, so I told her I'd scribble it in and if it proved impossible I'd call her back."

"Did she say what it was about?"

"Of course not. Do you think she would confide in a secretary? Do you want me to cancel, rearrange or what?"

"I can't stand Cahill."

"I know," Samantha sympathised.

"What do we know about her?"

"Ambitious but second rate. Straight from university and into politics. Never visited the real world. No business or other connections, as far as I am aware."

"How on earth did she get this number?"

"Maybe she got it from Adam Chandler. They say that they're close."

Slater shook his head, "No, she's just a useful idiot. Chandler wouldn't do that without telling me. He can't stand her."

"Do you want to see her?"

Slater shrugged. "Yes, I'm vaguely intrigued."

"Anything else?"

"Yes, bring me the boundary commission draft report."

He switched on the breakfast news with a notion that one of the features might alert him to Cahill's business, but none of the revelations proved out of the ordinary – just slightly depressing as he was forced to sit through the sports news and listen to an unconcerned English broadcaster re-tell the story of a European defeat for Manchester United. He silenced the box. Five minutes to eight. He didn't know much about Cahill, but he was sure that she would be on time.

There was a knock on the door and Sam brought in Sheila Cahill. Cahill was undeniably smart of appearance, the dark skirt and jacket of her business suit well-fitting and the rest of her appearance ordered and efficient, but somehow the overall effect was imperfect and unsatisfactory. She seemed a little more heavily made-up than the last time he had seen her. He got up to greet her. "Good morning, Sheila. Have a seat."

She sat down and he joined her at the mini-boardroom table.

"Coffee?"

"Yes, please."

The coffee arrived.

"Bob, I wanted to see you at once, for this is a matter of great delicacy and importance to the party. And," she added conspiratorially, "I need you to understand that this matter is highly confidential. So much so that if any word gets out, I'll deny everything. I wanted to talk to you because I know that you've got your finger on the pulse."

Did she have one? he wondered.

"The thing is that the prime minister …"

"Are you acting for him?"

"No, not exactly. This matter concerns him, I'm afraid. I'm acting on behalf of the party."

She moved a little closer and looked at him hard, raising the conspiratorial atmosphere up a level. "You see, unfortunately there have emerged, er, certain details about the PM which, if they were to become public, could seriously prejudice his position. I wanted to discuss this with you. Get a bit of advice."

"What details?"

She was coy now, almost arch. "Well, the details are a bit unclear at the moment and, in fact, might amount to nothing; however, it's always best to plan ahead. The party's been out of power for a long time and now that we're here, well, we can't allow anything to happen." She added, "No one's bigger than the party."

Bob knew many who were bigger than the Party – everyone in his address book – but he kept these thoughts to himself. He said blandly, "You really haven't told me much. Do you want me to do something?"

Cahill demurred. "No, not at all. Everything necessary is being done at present. I just wanted to talk with you about the future or, at least, one possible future."

Slater leant back a bit. This was interesting. Unusually, he didn't have a clue what was coming next. It was a novel feeling.

She went on, "Now, supposing that the PM felt that for the good of the Party and, of course, the country," she added as an afterthought, "he felt it necessary to step down. Now, in this unlikely event, how would you see the next steps: the best course for the party?"

"Why on earth would Adam have to stand down?"

"But if he had to stand down?"

"Okay, Sheila, I'll play your game. In this unlikely event, well, it's usually best that any period of uncertainty is as short as possible."

Cahill nodded vigorously. "Yes, exactly. Now, for that to happen, it will be prudent to engage in a certain amount of planning: contingency planning, of course. Organisational things like a base, preferably near the Commons. Equipped with phone lines and with enough space to plan strategy and win over wavering MPs."

He said incredulously, "Are you asking for the use of this office in the event of a leadership contest?"

"Well, let's say enquiring into its availability in the event it is required."

Slater couldn't help himself. "On whose behalf?"

Cahill smiled. "Bob, you're on the boards of many of our top companies, on committees and in daily touch with all the right people. What sort of person do you think we would need?"

"Someone who promises continuity. Enterprise-minded or, at least, not inclined to increase taxes or planning restrictions. In short, no real change. The present government was elected very recently, so we can risk the assumption that the country's happy to give them a run. There seems no reason to change policy direction."

Cahill pursed her lips. "Obviously no change in direction, but maybe a bit more focus on some areas."

"Like what?"

"Social issues, more kindness in our messaging. That sort of thing."

Slater managed to suppress a laugh but nodded as if in agreement. He had no desire to willingly subject himself to a series of ill-considered, juvenile lectures from Cahill.

Mercifully she moved on. "And would the right person have credibility problems if that person was perceived as being close to a disgraced prime minister?"

Slater ventured, "That would depend upon the nature of the disgrace, how personal to the PM it was. If it was purely personal to the PM, I doubt that current close associates would be tainted." He was firmer now. "But this is surely hypothetical nonsense?"

But Cahill couldn't be deflected. "But what of the right person – what other qualities would they need?"

Slater sighed. "I would say we would need a credible candidate who projects confidence and stresses business as usual. Really all the qualities that Adam has."

"We've had two women prime ministers; do you think we're ready for another?"

Christ, she was after it herself. A more unappealing candidate he could not imagine but, in reality, what were his objections? She probably fitted the broad description of suitable candidates he had already blandly described but stacked against this was a single overwhelming objection. He just didn't like her. So what? Pliability not likeability was the first consideration. Probably she would be cheap, but could she win?

"Why not?" he heard himself say.

"Yes, exactly," Cahill agreed. "So, Bob, in the event of such a turn of events, would you be in a position to help out?"

"Look, you've told me nothing."

"But if something were to happen?"

"Yes, I should give it serious consideration; however, this conversation has really gone as far as it can at this stage. Will you tell me what has happened to Adam?"

She tightened her lips. "I appreciate this is a strange discussion, Bob, and, like you, I hope that my fears are misplaced. Sufficient to say, I have received reports of some serious allegations against Adam. Like you, I am hopeful that they are inaccurate, malicious, nothing in them, but, on behalf of the party, I must ensure that we are prepared for every eventuality."

"Can you tell me the nature of these allegations?" Slater again asked.

"Look, it's serious, Bob. There's too many to detail. Sexual misconduct and more worryingly corruption dealings. Bribes, government favours for some dubious individuals. I can't say more at the moment, but I'll have everything finalised in a few days."

"A few days?"

"Yes, that's why I needed to speak to you urgently."

"How did you find out about all this?"

"Speaking to people. Good research. I'll explain everything when we meet next week."

Slater gave up. It was all he was going to get.

Cahill got up and extended a hand. "Well, thanks for your time and trouble, Bob. I'll see you next week. I'll let your assistant know the date and time."

He shook her hand with unenthusiastic professionalism and, a moment later, she was out of his office. Slater resumed his seat behind the desk, tilted his head skywards and shut his eyes. The voice of Sam dragged him away from the nightmare.

"Anything I can do?"

"Yes."

His phone buzzed. "Bob, I have the prime minister on the line."

Chapter 17

Having secured a couple of double brandies and a reclusive spot in the club, Bob Slater was ready for his meeting with the prime minister.

Chandler slid into a cavernous armchair. "Okay, Bob. What's so urgent?"

"Sheila Cahill came to see me today."

"So you said."

"And that doesn't bother you?"

"Why should it?"

"I would say it should when she talks about your imminent replacement as prime minister."

Chandler smiled complacently. "Ambition's a wonderful thing."

"Adam, you need to take this seriously."

"Why? Everything's under control."

"Not according to her."

Chandler had another mouthful of brandy. He laid down the glass and sighed. "What's she been saying?"

"She says she has uncovered troubling information about you personally. What can she mean?"

Chandler shook his head. "I really don't have an idea."

"She was talking about personal indiscretions."

"You know all about that, Bob. It's over with Alexis."

"Yes, but that's not all. She mentioned other things, corruption and bribes."

Chandler put his brandy down. "Any specifics?"

"No, thank goodness. But she was very confident."

"She's always confident."

"Who has she been speaking to recently?"

"No one that I know. Everything's normal."

"She was very confident," Slater repeated.

Chandler said, "We had MI5 in yesterday."

"Christ! What did they want?"

"Relax, it was just routine. About our recent high-profile accidents."

"And what do they think about that?"

"Not much. Just unfortunate accidents. They agreed we could put out a statement to that effect."

"And they only talked about Allardyce and Patterson?"

"Mostly."

"What else?"

"There was some talk about some letter received at party headquarters saying I was not fit to be prime minister."

"They think this is something to do with these deaths?"

"No, I don't think so. It was raised as an afterthought."

Slater gazed skywards. "Does Cahill know about this note?"

"No, she saw it today for the first time."

"Are you sure?"

"As far as I know. I caught the end of the meeting and I spoke to Sheila afterwards."

Slater said, "Who came from MI5? Anyone we know?"

"A brunette, mid-thirties. Good-looking. Amanda Barratt. I think I've seen her a couple of times at the Joint Security meetings, but I don't know much about her. Do you?"

"I've heard of her. They say she's a bit of a maverick, but a favourite of Nick Devoy. She's not usually the go-to resource for routine enquiries."

"Well, it was all pretty routine. Surely you expected people like that to poke their noses in when there's been a couple of deaths?"

"I suppose so, but how much does Cahill really know about you?"

"She thinks she's close, but she knows nothing about anything that's worth knowing."

"What about your business arrangements?"

"Of course not."

"No loose ends?"

"No."

"No one talking or feeling the need to get things off their chest."

"No one."

Slater looked at Chandler closely. "Adam," he said slowly, "you would tell me? I mean if you needed help with anything else."

"Yes, of course, Bob, but I don't."

"Cahill seemed so certain, so sure of herself," Slater repeated.

"I've told you. She's always certain."

"Are notes like that common?"

"We get dozens a day. Every day. Remember, about twelve million people didn't vote for me."

"I don't like it. We have got a lot of important work pending."

Chandler laughed. "Don't worry, the spending plans are already approved in draft. There's no problem, no changes. I've told you that."

"Yes, you've told me that."

"Don't worry, Bob, you've backed the right horse."

"I hope so, Adam. But people will become nervous."

"Tell them not to be."

Slater tried again. "Cahill was deadly serious. She was talking about taking over."

Chandler laughed loudly. "Look, Sheila has done a good job for the party, but she's talking nonsense. I mean how can she think that she's leadership material?"

"Yes, it's incredible. But the point is, why would she even think that you're on the way out?"

"Look, Bob, relax. All she's got is ambition. Cahill's got absolutely no support in the party. They see her as a necessary evil. I get delegations every week from ministers asking me to sack her."

Slater shook his head. "Cahill's done a lot for you, Adam, and she could be politically dangerous. Is there nothing we can do to shut her down?"

Chandler spat out. "She's done a lot for herself, Bob. Fucking parasite. She couldn't make it herself, so she latched on to someone who could. She seriously believes that I wouldn't have made it without her. Special adviser – hardly special – just spouts the sort of right-on shite that hundreds of others do. She's hardly ever earned a vote herself, yet she thinks that none of this could have happened without her."

Slater said, "You need to calm down. Don't lose your temper, it's bad tactics. Let's agree she's insignificant and she's probably all the things you say, but be careful, for God's sake. If you're in the clear, just leave it at that and ease her out. Promote her if that's what it takes. I'm told she's been hanging around with a journalist, Patrick Lawrence. God knows what she's told him."

"Lawrence is one of her favourites. I think she's got a sweet spot for him. How do you know that?"

"I've been asking around. Lawrence has broken one or two decent stories."

"Well, there isn't one here." Chandler leant forward. He wasn't laughing now. "Don't worry about Cahill, I'll deal with her. She actually thinks that she's in control, but she'll find out that she's not if she tries anything." He put down his brandy. "Look, Bob, I've a few things to do. I need to go. Don't worry."

Slater watched him leave. Long confident strides. Adam was an impressive man. A man always in control.

Slater reached for his phone. He was worried.

Chapter 18

Sheila Cahill was mostly satisfied with her meeting with Bob Slater. If the industrial fixer had not exactly jumped for joy, he had at least offered no objection to her potential ascension. She told herself that progress had been made. Then she had to repeat it to herself. A vague feeling of unease, an alien feeling that, somehow, she was being controlled and not in control. She expelled the thought. It was ridiculous. She determined the line on most of the major political stories and invariably read that line unalloyed and unchallenged in the morning editions. She was in control, no doubt about that.

Thursday was typically a slack day for government business, with most of the movers and shakers heading out of town, so Sheila had taken the reasonable but unusual decision to award herself the rest of the day off.

She was walking against the commuters, now close to the Bloomsbury district, where she owned a small flat.

The day was pleasant and birds were singing in the improbably green parks just yards from the teeming London thoroughfare. For a few steps she temporarily left the murky world of politics and drank in simpler pleasures. The noise of the traffic dimmed as she approached the Church of the Virgin, incongruously situated down a narrow alleyway with flats and houses all around. The church dated back to medieval times, yet was still at the heart of affairs for a diminishing, but devoted, band of local middle-class Roman

Catholics. Sheila had once been a Catholic but that was a long time ago. Nowadays, her apostasy had overwhelmed all traces of her meagre faith.

She knew why she had lost her faith. Mostly it was God's fault. He had let her down, denying her beauty and allowing her parents to die well before their time. After their deaths, she had drifted away from religion, and the break with the Catholic church had come as she had mulled over the improbabilities of papal infallibility. It wasn't that the concept of infallibility was incredible, but just that it was vested in the wrong man.

She passed the little church and a short, pleasant walk through the park took her to her home. When she entered the second-storey two-bedroomed flat, the view was as she had left it. In her bay-windowed drawing-room with its modern and functional appointments, she risked upsetting the delicate balance by throwing down her leather briefcase on the carpet and proceeding back through the hall and into her bedroom.

It was a large, bright room, sparsely and tastefully appointed, and home to a large oak-framed double bed, a dresser, chair and wardrobe. Through another door, she emerged into her favourite room: her en-suite dressing room. This was the largest space in the small flat. It had meant giving up two smaller rooms to create, but there had always been only her, so what did it matter?

She changed quickly, and, while still improving her hair and make-up, the bell rang. He was early.

He looked good. Tall and strong. Still casually dressed, but there were small signs that he had made an effort.

She said in a soft voice, "Thanks for coming, Patrick. Come in. There's much to discuss. Sorry I'm a bit disarranged, but I was a bit late myself. Can I get you a drink?"

"Scotch and water."

She mixed drinks for them both and sat opposite. She crossed her legs. He looked. That was good, but business first. "Now, Patrick. I promised you an exclusive and I've got one. As I said earlier, a scandal that goes right to the top."

"So far all I've heard about is a note, some possible sexual misadventures and unspecified corruption. We need much more, if you are serious."

"I'm deadly serious. I've not been idle. I've spoken to some of the party's key sponsors. They were very supportive."

"Supportive of what?"

"Me taking over." She delved into a briefcase and again produced that tantalising buff folder, which she skimmed through. "I've got a list of dozens of partners in the last few years. Adam is incredibly indiscreet. All ages, all sexes."

"Can you prove it?" Lawrence enquired.

"Yes, it's all here."

"Okay, so we've got the perfect family man. And a long-standing, long-suffering loyal wife. At least a double print run. Is he still at it?"

"Does a leopard change its spots?"

Lawrence said matter-of-factly, "Good, but you mentioned corruption, blackmail, and government favours. Sexual indiscretions just won't do it. The public like Chandler, so they'll forgive him a lot."

"Maybe."

"Definitely. Remember Alan Clarke?"

"Before my time, but I've got so much more."

"I need to hear it."

Cahill again delved into the folder, and after a moment selected a single leaf, which she handed across. "What do you think of that? It details an award of a government contract a few years ago and a payment of fifty thousand pounds."

"We need proof."

"I've got witnesses, dates and times. I've got the money trail."

"And you can link it to Chandler?"

She beamed. "I can."

"How many more of these things?"

"More than a dozen. Here's another. Two hundred thousand pounds for a couple of knighthoods. And the next one is a big one. Five hundred thousand pounds to facilitate an illegal consignment of military technology out of the country."

Lawrence read the brief details. "And you say you have a dozen similar things?"

"More than that."

"Hmm, that's a lot of information. How can you carry out investigations like this? This smells like the work of the security services. I won't play the patsy for them."

"Relax, they know nothing about this. It's all my own work."

"Hard to believe, to be honest. Surely you had help?"

"A little from researchers, but they don't know the whole story."

"You trust the researchers?"

"Yes, they think the research is for a book."

"Who are the researchers?"

"That doesn't matter. I know what I'm doing. Really, the research was easy. You know what they say."

"What do they say?"

"Follow the money, of course."

Lawrence made to speak but Cahill got in first. "So, can Chandler survive this?"

"Not if you have the proof."

"I do. Furthermore, I know about his next deal. Let me tell you."

Lawrence sat forward.

"A week or so ago, in the late evening, I was in my office. There was a large reception going on, but I was too busy to go. Anyway, my office is linked to Downing Street, and Chandler burst in. He seemed surprised to see me and asked that I give up my room for a few minutes while he had an off-the-record chat with some ambassador. At this meeting, Chandler agreed to arrange for the importation of some goods and to pay a large amount of money in return for the man's silence. It was even suggested that this wasn't the first time."

"Did you see who it was?"

"No, but I heard every word."

"You listened at the door?"

"Not exactly."

"Pity … if it's something that only you heard, then we only have your word. Not exactly cast iron."

"True, very true," Cahill agreed. She leant forward and delivered the coup de gras. "However, the recording is."

Lawrence looked skyward, and over his thumping heart said, "You've got a recording?"

She looked triumphant. "I have."

"Is your office bugged?"

"Of course not. You read too many spy novels. Actually, I would like to claim all the credit but, in reality, it was a lucky accident. I was dictating letters at the time. My phone was in my desk and everything happened so quickly I forgot to switch it off."

"How good's the recording?"

"Clear as a bell."

"Can I hear it?"

"Later," she continued self-importantly, "After I listened to the recording, I spent a great deal of time thinking. As you know, I am a great supporter of the prime minister; however, our programme and policies are more important than any individual. So, it is my duty to act. Of course, any public scandal will inevitably affect the government, and this is the thing we must avoid."

Lawrence said, "But when this story breaks, it's bound to reflect on the party."

"Not necessarily. I have a way to get this done."

"Go on."

"Obviously Adam has to go, and, given what I know, that is the easy part."

"And you will use the threat of publication to achieve it?"

"Yes, but in a way that doesn't hole the government below the waterline. This needs to be pinned on Adam the individual."

Lawrence shook his head. "If this becomes public, then the police, everyone, will be involved."

"Yes, but if Adam just unexpectedly resigns, obviously there'll be a clamour to know why, but I can spin any number of bland explanations. More time with his wife, bad health, something like that."

"But when we publish the story?"

"There is no reason for everything to come out immediately."

"Well, what's in it for me?"

Cahill leant forward and tapped him on his hand. "Plenty, but you need to be just a little patient. I'll give you everything, but you have to wait a little. Every conspiracy theorist in the country will be in a frenzy. Why did Chandler resign? You wait a while, I give you all the details, then your book comes out, maybe serialised in your newspaper."

"There's money in that certainly, but how long do I have to wait?"

"The next election's about four years away. I take over, we win, and then you can publish everything."

"If you want a long delay, why do you need me?"

Cahill looked at him. "Obviously to convince Adam that if he doesn't resign and help me, things will come out immediately."

"You'd do that?"

"It would be my duty, as I see it."

Lawrence said, "And if he calls your bluff?"

"All we need to do is curate the stories, manage the timing carefully and control the process. There's a lot of strings that Adam can pull when he's still in post. This way gives us the best chance of a smooth changing of the guard. Maintain confidence in the country. But don't worry. Adam will go, I promise you that."

Lawrence sipped at his whisky. "Yes, I can quite see that, but we need to move quickly."

"Of course."

"What about these recent deaths?"

"Nothing to do with this, Patrick, I'm sure of that. Patterson fell off his balcony, drunk probably."

"And Allardyce?"

"Another accident. Forget him. What can it have to do with this?"

"Nothing, I was just thinking that if the police are poking about, maybe it would be better if we sped things up. You could give me a copy of everything you've got. I'll get our lawyers all over it in an hour. We can do everything off the record – with total secrecy."

Cahill shook her head. "Don't worry. We do need to move fast, but we aren't ready for that yet. I need a little time to organise things. If you come round here tomorrow evening, I'll have everything ready. Be on time, but no lawyers, just you."

"Fine, see you then."

Lawrence hadn't been on time for a meeting since high school, but he knew that this time, he would be.

Chapter 19

Alexis Patterson sat alone in her drawing-room and barely registered an emotion as her father entered the room.

"Hi, Lexi. Drink?"

"Yes, a small one."

He sat alongside her and squeezed her hand. "How was your day?"

"All right."

"You sure?"

"Not really. They spiked my story."

"Hardly surprising. Your beloved prime minister is bought and paid for. Did you think your proprietor would allow serious criticism of Chandler?"

"It was a fair article. All true."

"Dear Lexi, don't you ever learn?"

"It seems not, but what can I do?"

"Nothing. Forget everything. Move on."

"Move on to where?"

"Come and help me with the party. We need all the help we can get."

Alexis laughed. "Well, you're right about that. Why don't you give it up?"

"What would I do?"

"I don't know, but it's a lost cause."

"Well, there are a few challenges, it's true, but the party's doing well, and we've got great hopes for the council elections. I think that with one push at local level, we can get the party back on the right track. The thing is, Alexis, there's one or two expenses which need to be met for the campaign and I was hoping for a bit of short-term help. Just, er, until one or two donations come in."

Alexis laughed. "Always just one more push. The party's finished. Why won't you recognise that and move on?"

"We had 10% in a poll in the Standard the other day."

"You once had nearly 25%."

"And we will again," Hamilton protested.

Alexis took his hand. "No, you won't. They will never allow that."

Hamilton's cheeks flushed. "Alexis, please, look – it's just for a few weeks until I get a few things sorted out. Could you manage twenty thousand?"

"Barely, Colin's left me rather badly off."

"I'll get it back. I promise."

Alexis Patterson looked at her father. She kissed him on the cheek. "Christ, I miss Suffolk. We were happy there."

"Yes, we were. I've let you down, Lexi. I've blown five hundred years of work."

"You did what you thought was right."

"I didn't think enough."

"What can we do?" Alexis lamented.

Hamilton sat up. "We'll be fine. Our family always endures. That's what we do."

Alexis sighed. "My chequebook's in my bag."

Chapter 20

After his meeting with Amanda Barratt, John McMahon sat alone in the solitary chair in his bedsit – a single room measuring little more than a couple of hundred feet square, but more than enough for his few possessions. He picked up an empty noodle container and laid it down on the side of the sink after failing to find space in an overflowing black binbag. He reviewed numerous plates and dishes caked with food well past the sell-by date. There was no rush. He could clear things up later, so he repaired to his only chair, rakishly placed in the centre of the room, and lit a cigarette. That was better; the tobacco smoke masked all the other competing smells.

He had been the occupant of this unprepossessing dwelling for about three months and, despite its inadequacy and squalor, to McMahon it did not represent rock bottom. As an alternative to street life, it was a leg up the social ladder.

McMahon stared at the grimy, green-tinged linen sheet that covered the single window. How quickly things changed, he mused. One moment decorating the Earl's Court flat, making plans, patronising fancy restaurants and galleries … and then, within a year, disaster.

At first David's illness had been manageable, and while he stayed fit and healthy, all was well. But gradually David's constitution had faltered and, with his illness, pretty soon customers became former customers.

The business had folded as quickly as it had grown and then the flat was gone and then came David's requirement for twenty-four-hour care. When he had finally been committed to hospital without hope of release, McMahon had gone to pieces and had tried, and failed, several times to kill himself. He had lacked the courage to, in turn, propel himself from Southwark Bridge, stay motionless in the face of an oncoming train and, finally, make a deep enough incision in his wrist with a rusty penknife. The marks from this last failed attempt were still visible on his emaciated wrists.

That was about three months ago, so maybe things were on the up. On any measure, life was still rotten, but somehow his recent adventures, and even the brush with the all-too-realistic face of British Intelligence, had cheered him up.

It was true that he was under threat of being charged with attempted blackmail, but McMahon thought this unlikely and, even better, after the interview the woman had given him a hundred pounds. Things were looking up. He counted all of the notes carefully and put them on the table alongside another small pile of notes.

He fell heavily onto his chair and recklessly lit his last cigarette. With his recently acquired wealth, he contemplated what now would be a decent evening.

In response to a loud, unexpected knock, he forced himself out of the chair, still considering this happy prospect.

McMahon didn't get many visitors these days, but he was on a roll, and he opened the door with something approaching enthusiasm.

The corridor was dimly lit and McMahon was pretty sure that he didn't know his visitor.

He didn't invite him inside either, but the visitor didn't wait for an invitation, and a moment later McMahon was flying backwards into his room. An inky blackness descended before his eyes. A moment later the blackness became total and eternal, and McMahon's suffering ended for ever.

Chapter 21

Today, Jack had met the prime minister and some other public figures and conducted surveillance through the city streets. Action-packed to some, but tedious for Jack, save in an important respect: his time with Amanda. He looked forward to her visiting later as she had promised, after heading to her office, leaving him to walk back to his London home, another thing he had little enthusiasm for.

Nowadays, he spent nearly all of his free time in Mascar in the Scottish Highlands, and each time he visited the capital the contrast between the two places became more pronounced and increasingly in favour of the Highland retreat. His financial advisers had recommended that a balanced investment portfolio was an absolute necessity. As the property had almost doubled in value over the last two years, he grudgingly acknowledged they had been proved correct, but what did a balanced portfolio have to do with an enjoyable life?

As he approached the steps of the mansion flat in the Georgian parade, he conceded that if he must come to London then it was far more comfortable than the hotels of the capital.

He entered the block and nodded at an efficient concierge who, despite the infrequency of his visits, always recognised him. Overcome with exhaustion, he opted for the lift in preference to the stairs to gain the single floor.

The flat was big, far too big, consisting of some seven or eight rooms, each of which was high-ceilinged and expensively furnished.

The elegance of the furnishings was little to do with him, however, but the effect was pleasing. In a moment of madness, he had left an open cheque with an interior designer. As he deserved, with this sort of project management the bill had been eye-watering. An "investment", they had said.

Most concurred that the designer had done a good job, but to Jack it still didn't feel like his home, and each visit saw him creeping round the furniture, silently apologising if he used the house too roughly.

After a walk around the flat to check that all was in order, he had a quick shower, put on a heavy robe and retired to the only room in the flat in which his designer had decided that a television could tastefully be housed. He switched on the screen on the wall and adjusted his eyes to get used to the cinema-screen size of the contraption. The news was on and it was boring.

A feature about the prime minister appointing a new party chairman briefly engaged him, but he tired of it quickly when a sycophantic BBC journalist gushed in tribute to the PM's decisive step in emphasising business as usual. The BBC loved Chandler, and Jack wondered why. He had met the man today and, as far as Jack was concerned, he was bland and talentless. Surely others felt the same?

He switched off the TV and shut his eyes.

Not for long. The doorbell rasped.

He opened the door. Amanda was early.

"How did you get up here? Is the concierge not around?"

"Yes, he's there."

"And he let you up without buzzing me?"

"He's an old friend."

"Do you know everyone in London?"

"Not everyone. Can I come in?"

"Yes, sorry. Drink?"

"Yes thanks."

"Any progress?"

Her head dropped very slightly, and her voice was unusually light. "Not much."

This wasn't the Amanda he knew, looked up to, maybe even loved. Where was superwoman?

"Is everything OK?"

"Yes, I'm fine."

He flopped on the sofa beside her. "OK, what's up?"

"Oh, nothing really, I just hate dealing with politicians."

"Don't you have to deal with them all the time?"

"Yes, and I'm sick of it."

"It goes with the turf. Have another drink."

"Just a small one. I've been thinking about quitting, you know?"

"Quitting?"

"Yes."

"You can't quit."

"Why not?"

"Because you can't."

She smiled. "Well, I'm glad we've cleared that up."

"Look, if you quit, all these fuckers will keep getting away with God knows what."

Amanda said, "So I'm all that's standing in the way of the fall of the Empire?"

"Yes, something like that."

"Doubtful, but it's just that everything is so crap … everything so perverted. Every day, squalor, murder, greed, and I'm sick and I'm tired of it all. If there's evil, then there must be good …" She raised her voice several decibels. "But where's the fucking good?"

He put his hand on her arm. "Hey, this is not you." He lit two cigarettes and gave her one. "You're the professional. It's me that's meant to be like this."

She laughed a bit. "I'm fine really. Just meeting that guy today."

"McMahon?"

"Yes, I mean, what's he got? It seems so unfair."

"Maybe," Jack agreed.

"It's not really the type of thing a hardened investigator should think."

"I don't agree," Jack said. You can't do your job by numbers. You've got to have a bit of humanity." He brushed her arm lightly. "And, you have – that's what makes you good."

She squeezed his arm back, and they sat in silence for a moment before she said, "If I chucked it, maybe we could spend more time together. Don't you want that?"

Jack's heart leapt. "What a question."

"A difficult question?"

"Let's say it's tough to cram an answer into a soundbite."

"Good. I've had enough of soundbites."

Another silence, except for Jack's whirring brain.

"OK, here goes," he said. "You're the most important person in my life. Now that might be because I've got no one else or it might be because I love you. As for your job, that's difficult also. You're great at it, but it's dangerous. So, in summary, I worry about coming on too strong and losing you as a friend, and I worry about losing you to an assassin's bullet. I guess I'm just a worrier. That's a long speech for me."

"But not too bad," Amanda said. She leant across and kissed him. This felt quite good, so Jack tried it a few more times. "Do you need to go soon?"

She turned to him and looked at him with big eyes. "No rush."

The rising insistent rasp of the mobile phone seemed several thousand light years distant, and then so near that it couldn't be ignored. Amanda disengaged and stared at the phone. "Fuck off," she said to it, but it couldn't be ignored.

After some listening, superwoman was back. She put on her coat. "Sorry, you'll have to get dressed."

Chapter 22

Although the taxi ride to the Paddington district took over fifteen minutes in the unyielding traffic, they had uttered not a word during the journey, which was annoying for Jack. He felt vulnerable. He had told Amanda quite a few important things.

When they alighted from the taxi, the rain was falling lightly and the night was moonless and black, or at least it would have been had it not been for the white, red and yellow tongues of fire dancing out of the roof of the tenement building.

Jack stood mesmerised while Amanda located those in charge and engaged in a brief conversation with a fire officer before re-joining him a few minutes later.

"Well, what's up now?" he asked.

"A fire, obviously, but luckily the fire brigade got on top of it fairly early. It seems that the worst is over and there's no structural damage."

He felt utterly fed up and resented deeply the fact that they were here rather than back at the flat. "So, that's all right then. What on earth are we here for?"

Her voice was ice cold now. "This is where John McMahon lives. A bedsit on the top floor. The fire chief thinks the fire might have started there."

Jack felt sick. "Tell me McMahon's not in there?"

She shrugged. "I can't. I don't know. It'll take a while for the stairwells to be cleared and then we'll see."

"He'll be there, I just know it."

Amanda's head bowed a bit.

"Fuck, if only we had picked him up earlier."

She snapped back, "Don't you think I know that?"

He took her arm, "Sorry, I know. Do you want a coffee?"

"Yes, thanks."

Amanda moved off again, joining a gaggle of officials, and Jack drifted off in search of coffee. London was a town that never slept, and even at this hour there was usually no shortage of choice. He reminded himself of this truth as he walked about a quarter of a mile without success, and he was still reminding himself when he caught sight of the giant railway terminus. At least they would have coffee there.

The concourse was buzzing as always. Tramps begging, some bedding down for the night, drunken city workers conducting illicit after-work petting sessions, and a large throng of frustrated commuters crowded around a large noticeboard telepathically urging it to update its information with better news.

After ten minutes in a queue and giving over most of a ten-pound note, he had two black coffees of modest size. He turned to head back to the smouldering apartment block but was stopped in his tracks as he caught sight of a man he had seen before.

The man was sitting with three others inside the coffee bar at an uncomfortable-looking plastic table. As Jack stared, the man flashed a simultaneous glance. Jack looked away, but for a fraction of a second their eyes met. Jack wasn't usually good with faces, but even he could remember someone he'd met earlier today.

He wondered what St John, Lord Hamilton, peer of the realm, could be discussing with three youngish men of dubious appearance at this time of night. The contrast was certainly acute, for while Lord Hamilton was clad from head to toe in high quality apparel – a pinstripe suit, expensive shoes and a heavy, good quality overcoat – the others wore jeans and street-style jackets.

He lost sight of the group as a harassed traveller, having finally had his much-delayed train called, rushed past and nearly knocked him over. Jack shouted a few X-rated words into the night air and then straightened himself slowly. He looked back to the coffee bar but the assembled party had left. He shook off a few spots of scalding coffee from his hand, surveyed the scene and was rewarded by a fleeting glance of the group heading out of the station.

Most of the coffee was lying dangerously on the already treacherous station concourse, so he threw both cartons in the bin and headed back to the coffee bar. The queue was even longer now, and as he waited, he was suddenly overtaken by a ridiculous notion. He turned and looked up and, satisfied that he could still make out the men through the throng, he decided to follow them.

As he walked, he kept asking himself why he was doing this. Each time an unknown answer satisfied his subconscious and he continued to tail them from a discreet distance.

At first it was easy. The people on the busy streets made a perfect camouflage, but after a few minutes and after turning a few corners, the throng thinned. Jack increased his pace to close the distance but needed to be careful as the route took in narrower and quieter routes, eventually turning into something that looked like a lane. Jack didn't follow them round the corner, instead waiting a moment before edging his head round to take in the scene.

It was a long alleyway that looked like a dead end, but eventually it made a circular route from the station and underneath one of the main railway lines. Despite the poor-quality coverage from a single orange streetlight some hundred yards along the cobbled alley, Jack could see all he needed to form a general picture. The alley was home to a terrace of low-rent units and workshops and, although it seemed to go on forever, his attention was drawn to an open door at one of the units about halfway down.

All was quiet, and at first there was no sign of the men as he nosed around the corner, but as he had further thoughts of giving up this pointless exercise, a figure briefly emerged and then returned to a lock-up, dragging the door over irregular stony ground and slamming it shut.

Jack stood rigid against the wall, his thumping heart louder than a roaring train. With the men safely secured within in the unit, what now?

Time to call off this minor and unplanned adventure. That would have been easy, safe and sensible. He re-checked the alley and then, with calculated strides, moved forward until he stood outside the door.

The two-leaf wooden door was sturdy, but in indifferent condition. One of the leaves contained a cut-out wicket entry door. There were no windows, and the thickness of the doors and the rising breeze at first seemed to rule out the possibility of overhearing anything from inside. As his senses acclimatised, he found that this wasn't quite true. The imperfect setting of the two leaves allowed a small, but adequate, slit. The wind died, and he could hear the sound of voices now, although the words could not be discerned. He took his ear away and pressed his eye to the gap.

He couldn't see anything, so he went back to listening. He strained hard with his ears, but the intermittent wind was maddening and the sound volumes went up and down before the deafening roar of a train overhead obliterated them completely.

When the train and its aftershock had disappeared into the distance, he steeled himself for a further effort, which seemed to be working, for the voices seemed louder, yet maddeningly no clearer. His senses were adapting, but that wasn't what was increasing the volume. He sprang back from the door. It was time to go, but Jack stood immobile. A lock clicked, louder than a starter pistol, and he sprinted back around the corner, nearly bursting his out-of-condition lungs. He didn't slow until he had reached the safety of the still-teeming station concourse. On regaining the crowd, his heart rate had stabled, and he returned to the coffee bar, ordered two black coffees and began a more relaxed walk back to the scene of the fire.

When he returned, progress had been made. Only one fire wagon and a skeleton staff remained, and the crowds of nosey parkers had been largely cleared. If Amanda was surprised that it had taken him forty-five minutes to get the drinks, she didn't say so and merely accepted the cup, took a mouthful and updated him on the situation.

"They're just about ready for us. The fire's out but we need to wait on the fire master before we can go up."

On cue the fire master joined them. "Okay, ma'am, you can go in."

Jack followed as Amanda led the way up blackened stairs, followed by two uniformed policemen. After three flights, they came to a small landing with two opposing doors. One was closed but the other was smashed in. Jack followed Amanda inside.

Before it had been razed it hadn't been much, and the flat hadn't been improved by the application of fire and water. It hadn't done much for McMahon either, and he sat on the floor, leaning against the drenched remains of a single bed, his face upturned and contorted in a hideous death mask.

Jack allowed himself a short glance at the body. McMahon didn't have much in life, and his luck hadn't changed in death. He wondered how Amanda would react, but for the moment she was in full business mode. He withdrew to the door while she conducted a careful examination of the tiny home, finally closely examining the dead body of McMahon. She rose from the examination looking pale and angry. She shouted to the constables, "Has he been moved?"

"Yes, ma'am. The firemen who broke down the door told me that they moved him onto the landing and tried to revive him, but he was dead, so they concentrated on the fire. Afterwards, they moved him back into the room." The constable, having finished his reply, turned around to face his colleague, and in response to an inaudible remark, his colleague smiled broadly.

Amanda's face froze. She stared at the constable. His smile vanished. She kept staring. Jack looked at her. He'd seen her kill people, but he had never seen her angrier.

Jack sidled alongside, took her arm and gently steered her back to the centre of the room. Surprisingly she didn't resist, and without a word refocused upon the room. She said, "Looks like that fat fryer there," indicating its charred remains.

"And the smoke got him?" suggested Jack.

"No. Nothing to do with the smoke. As far as I can see, someone snapped his neck." She made a gesture with her hands and added, "Just like a little twig. As for the chip pan, it may have been on when he was attacked, or, of course," and her tone suggested that this was a stronger probability, "the murderer could have decided to muddy the evidence."

"Does it take much to snap a neck? I mean, presumably it had to be a man?"

"No, look at him. About eight stone dripping wet – a man or woman could have done this, that is, if they knew the technique."

"Do you know the technique?"

"Yes."

An old-fashioned attitude surfaced, and Jack protested, "But surely it's a man's crime, this? Granted, a woman could do it, but …"

"But what?"

"Well, I don't really know."

Amanda said, "Statistically, you are correct. Women very rarely kill with their hands."

"Well, that's that."

"Maybe."

She turned back to the serious-faced constables. "How long before Therm gets here?"

One of the constables checked on a radio. "Doctor Therm will be here in a few minutes, ma'am."

There didn't seem much more to say, so they waited a few minutes until footsteps and voices could be heard approaching. A moment later a massive tweed-suited figure led about half a dozen people into the tiny bedsit.

Jack said, "Is that Therm?"

"Yes."

Therm acknowledged Amanda briefly, then, after a short meeting, sent his white-suited charges to their tasks. Jack and Amanda withdrew to the edge of the room as Therm and his assistants got to work. They worked quickly but without any sign of concluding, and after about ten minutes, Amanda interrupted. "Thomas, a word."

"Yes, Amanda?"

Amanda wasn't a television detective, so she didn't demand all the facts – just one. "Did someone break his neck?"

Luckily, Therm wasn't a TV pathologist either, so he trusted her with a provisional opinion. "I would say so, Amanda."

"Right. Thanks, I'll get the full report later."

"What are you doing here?"

"I'm interested, but just carry on as normal. Except for one thing."

"Which is?"

"Record this as a John Doe for the moment."

"Understood."

Jack said, "What now?"

"Just a minute." With deliberate head movements, Amanda conducted a last sweep of the small room. Then she stopped and seemed to alight on something on the far wall. She advanced back into the room and, after a word with one of the workers, removed a flyer and put it in her pocket.

Chapter 23

The crowd had dispersed when they returned to the street. Amanda was still business-like, but a bit of her earlier weariness was beginning to seep out.

"All right?" Jack asked her.

"I need a drink."

He needed one as well. Finding alcohol proved easier than coffee, and a few hundred yards up the street, the Victory Arms smelt good. They entered the tawdry Victorian throwback, and Jack ordered drinks and brought them to her at a corner table.

They both took long mouthfuls of gin.

Jack was bursting to tell her about his adventure, but they hadn't finished mourning McMahon. "What was that you took off the wall?"

She reached into her pocket and produced the flyer. It was titled: "Superior Catering Company." The contact phone number was underlined.

Jack saw what she was driving at. "What would McMahon want with this?"

"Well, that's what I wondered," she replied.

And then he addressed the elephant in the room. "Sorry to go back to it, but why did you not arrest McMahon today?"

"Yes, if I had he might be alive. And you said that I was good at my job."

"You are good."

"I was keeping him on a long leash. If you remember, I arranged a tail."

"And what happened to that?"

"They lost him."

"I thought these guys were professionals."

"I'll be mentioning that to them. Sheer complacency. They took one look at McMahon and thought it would be easy. Idiots. If there is one type that knows the street, it's a drug user. He lost them in Soho."

Jack said, "At least your theory that the blackmail note is central to these killings looks right. What other reason could there be for McMahon's death?"

"Any number of low possibilities," Amanda said.

"Like a botched drug deal."

"Something like that."

"But we're beyond coincidence now."

"I would say so. If the note's the link, then the allegations must be true."

"But it's ridiculous, so disproportionate. No one cares about sexuality these days, and if Chandler behaves like that, dozens of folks must know. Is everyone going to be murdered?"

Amanda laughed mirthlessly. "We have a lot of work to do."

Jack felt sick, and Amanda wore a weary expression. He squeezed her hand and she responded a bit.

He sat up with a start. "Damn, I forgot to tell you. When I went for coffee …"

"You were away a long time."

"I had to go to the railway station."

"Oh."

"Yes, and you'll never guess who I ran into?"

"I'm too tired to guess," Amanda said.

"Lord Hamilton," he announced dramatically.

She seemed underwhelmed. "And?"

He recounted his adventures, and it perked her up.

"Very interesting indeed. What number unit?"

Jack couldn't remember. He ventured, "About half a dozen units down an alley."

"The name of the alley?"

"Sorry."

Orthodoxy was restored now, with Jack now making all the mistakes. "Not cut out for this sort of thing, are you?" she chided. "You'd better show me."

"Do you think it's important?"

"I have no idea, but it might take my mind off this miserable business for a moment."

"Maybe it's got to do with this business?"

"Seems unlikely. Let's get out of here."

She got up and he followed. Just before he left, Jack looked back into the lightly patronised bar and, at a far corner table, saw someone else that he recognised and had recently met for the first time.

Chapter 24

It was after ten in the morning when Jack's eyes opened in the spacious bedroom of his London flat. The curtains were tightly shut, but there was sufficient light to tell him that he should be doing something. He got out of bed. For once, today he had a job. Not a difficult one, but a job, nonetheless. It was already eleven, so a slice of burnt toast and some black tea had to do before he emerged onto the congestion of the Marylebone Road.

He looked right and left. A telepathic cab driver screeched to a halt in front of him. "Where to, mate?"

"Queens Road, Paddington, please."

The London traffic was at its worst and the heat inside the cab oppressive, but more bearable than the unbreathable air outside, and he fidgeted in the seat, tempted to instruct the driver to stop anywhere. He persevered and concentrated on talking to himself about why he was going to Paddington.

A routine task, Amanda had said. Probably it was, if you knew the routine.

Ray Dewar: the red-haired girl in the Essex hotel where they had met Allardyce. Meeting someone once was normal, and maybe so was spotting them a few days afterwards in a pub. And maybe her living in a flat a few doors down from the luckless McMahon was another coincidence, but Amanda hadn't thought so.

Jack reviewed the text message again. A name, address, occupation – researcher – and a date of birth – thirty, as Jack had guessed. Not much information, but when you thought about it, not so easy to get, unless you worked for MI5.

The cab deposited him on the long busy street. He checked the numbers. Typically, he was at the wrong end of the street, but in better news, he had been dropped right next to the Victory Arms. Why not?

It had been half-empty last night, but it was packed to the rafters this lunchtime, and it was with difficulty that Jack forced himself to the bar and obtained an indifferent pint from an indifferent Australian bartender. By his third pint, the lunchtime patrons had virtually cleared the place and the Victory Arms had returned to its natural state, home only to a very drunken businessman who alternated between burying his head in his hands and removing them to down whiskies in a single mouthful, and a very old lady drinking a small bottle of stout very slowly whilst sitting with her legs splayed unappealingly allowing, from time to time, a far from tantalising view of what might have been pre-war nylons.

Jack downed his pint and yawned. Time for work. First, the gents. On his return, the scene was very much as before, save for the single important addition of an extremely attractive redhead who, in well-remembered tones, ordered a coffee. Dewar, for someone so young, was certainly a creature of habit, and he watched her at a corner table again wrestling with a broadsheet newspaper. He ordered another pint and a vodka and tonic and made his way over to her. She saw him approaching this time and threw the paper aside. Her face told of an inner struggle to place a face.

Being even imperfectly remembered was a start, and Jack felt unusually confident as he sat on a low iron-legged stool at her table and placed down the drinks. "Remember me? I'm the guy who buys you drinks in Essex."

Her face cleared. She smiled at him and said, "The man in the hotel."

"Jack Edwards, and you are …" He paused for effect – well, he didn't want to appear too keen – "Ray, is it?"

Ray Dewar smiled, flicked her thick red hair off her face and said conspiratorially, "So, we meet again, Mr Edwards. What a coincidence. What brings you to this dump?"

He said confidently, hardly believing the sound of his own voice, "Actually, I came in to see you."

Taken metaphorically, it certainly sounded cheesy, but she accepted it literally. "To see me? How on earth did you imagine you would see me?"

"I saw you last night."

"Yes, I often use this place for office work. It's never busy except for lunchtimes. I'm on coffee, of course."

"You live nearby?"

"Yes." She smiled at him again and said, "Well, now you've caught up with me, what now?"

Jack had to come clean. He flashed the warrant card. It always had the same effect. Her smile vanished. She sat up a little straighter and moved a little further away. "Is it about that man who died at the hotel?"

Detective work was easy. "Yes."

"I can't tell you anything. I just stopped in for a drink. I think I mentioned to you I was driving back to London that evening."

"I remember. The guy that died was called Phillip Allardyce. Did you know him?"

"Not exactly, but I had heard of him."

"Oh."

She continued, "I'm a researcher and I sometimes do political research. It's not really my speciality, but it sometimes pays the bills."

"You weren't doing any work with him?"

"Oh no. I had no idea he was at the hotel."

Jack said, "Sorry, but I need to ask the times that you arrived and left."

"Arrived about seven thirty and was away just after eight. One drink. Don't you need a pencil to write these things down?"

"I don't have one."

"Are you new at this game?" Dewar asked.

"Part-time."

"Have you any more questions?"

"Er, yes, a few, if you don't mind."

"Go ahead, but I thought the newspapers said that it was an accident?"

"Oh probably, but we have to check everything."

"I suppose so."

"Did you see anyone else that you recognised at the hotel? Maybe other political figures were around?"

"No, no one that I recognised, but as I've said, I was only in and out."

Jack said, "There was a fire just down the road last night."

"Yes, luckily nowhere near me." She lowered her voice. "They say a man was killed. Is that true?"

"Yes, I think so."

"What was his name?"

Jack wasn't sure what to say, so he played safe. "I don't know much about it. Don't you know? I mean, you're local."

"No such thing as local around here, Jack. I don't know anyone except the folks in this pub. These flats have a lot of coming and going. It's quite a rundown area. I'm hoping to get somewhere better soon, but I never seem to make enough money." Ray Dewar smiled. "Any more questions?"

"None that I can think of at the minute."

"Maybe you'll think of something later."

"Maybe."

"What about, say, a slightly longer meeting? Unless you have more work to do."

"Not much," he admitted. "What do you have in mind?"

She said, "Well, I've been meaning to go to the Tower of London. I'd like to see the birds there – the ravens."

"I love ravens, too. You ought to see them in the wild, tumbling and croaking. I've got a pair behind my house. They nest on the crags."

"In London?"

"No, up in Scotland. The north-west."

She looked at him and smiled. "I'd like to see that."

"Well, it's a bit far away, but we could go to the Tower. That's only about twenty minutes away by taxi."

Ray Dewar said, "I don't usually take taxis."

"I can manage that," Jack said.

It was an unlikely mutual interest to find, but it was a mutual interest, and, after they had finished their drinks, they taxied to the Tower.

Work wasn't all that bad, Jack thought, as he headed for what promised to be an enjoyable and easy afternoon ambling through the sinister portals of the Tower of London with a highly agreeable companion.

Chapter 25

While Jack was "questioning" Ray Dewar, Amanda was working hard, having borrowed an office at the local police station. McMahon's autopsy report consisted of two pages of A4 paper only. McMahon was as insignificant in death as he had been in life. Caucasian, male, about fifty years old. Cause of death: a broken neck inflicted by a person or persons unknown. There wasn't much more, and the pathologist seemed to care as little for McMahon as the rest of society. There were only a few sentences in the "additional observations" box, which stated that, while McMahon was superficially feeble, he was, underlyingly, in reasonable health; and the pathologist posited, for what it was worth, that if he had stopped taking drugs, he might have lived a normal span.

Detective Inspector Allan was in charge and was soon in Amanda's office. She introduced herself. Allan was a tall, spare man who looked close to retirement, but any thoughts she had that he would not give this case his best were soon dispelled. Allan was a democrat. He believed that every murder victim was equally important. "We've spoken to everyone in the block. A few admitted to having seen McMahon, but none to knowing him. Not really surprising to be honest, it's a transient area. Everyone's a stranger."

Amanda said, "What else?"

He opened a folder and read from a check list. "Bank account – no, credit card – no, online activity – no."

"Not much of a start?" Amanda teased.

"No, ma'am."

"The landlord?"

"McMahon's been a tenant for about a year or so, rent was about three weeks overdue. Apparently he had been saying that he was expecting money soon,"

"Figures. What else did the landlord know?"

"Nothing, ma'am. It's not the sort of establishment that is too particular about references."

Amanda said, "Is the landlord of any interest to us?"

"I'm keeping an eye on him, but I don't think so. We can make life uncomfortable for him if you want, but three weeks behind with the rent made McMahon one of his better tenants. I can't see him killing McMahon; besides, he was on holiday at the time."

"Where?"

"Portugal, he has a villa there."

"Naturally."

"Do you want me to dig further?"

"Oh, use your judgement. Now, what about that flyer?"

"The Superior Catering Company. Outside caterers, quite high class. They were around for about five years, but it stopped trading about a year ago. I have here accounts for the last three years." He handed her copies. "Very profitable business, profits in the millions. It closed about a year ago. A voluntary liquidation." Allan continued. "A single director, a David Ross."

"Who's David Ross?"

"I've not caught up with him yet. Last known address was given as Thames Lane, Earl's Court. Expensive place. The flat's now in the name of a Phillip Jones, who bought it a couple of years ago."

"Have you spoken to him?"

"Yes. He didn't know Ross, bought it through agents. Looks pretty standard to me."

Amanda picked up the accounts. "Have you talked to these accountants?"

"Not yet, ma'am. Is it important?"

Amanda sighed. "I've no idea what is important, to be honest. Keep going. I think I'll go and see these accountants."

Allan left the office and Amanda rang Max Harris and briefed him on her limited progress. "What I really want is to find out who McMahon was. And a man called David Ross." She looked at her notes and gave him Ross's last known address. "What can you do?"

"My best, boss."

She left it – Harris's best was usually good enough.

She needed air. She put on her jacket, but her office door resounded with a knock again.

"Come in."

Inspector Wilcox. He was an unlikely narcotics man. He was small and round and looked like a minor clerk from the 1950s. "This information on Lord Hamilton's night-time activity is interesting. We've had a look at the station CCTV. One of Hamilton's group was Jason Barnes."

Amanda whistled. She didn't keep up with the drugs trade, but everyone knew Barnes. "Well, if Barnes is involved it will be something big."

"Usually is," Wilcox agreed. "What do you want to do?"

"Have you information on anything imminent?"

"Nothing in particular, but Barnes is very active. What's a peer of the realm doing with Jason Barnes?"

Amanda said, "Who knows, but maybe the oldest story in the world. He's spent millions on that political party. Now it's out of money. Word is, so is he."

Wilcox looked at her. "So, what do you need?"

"Twenty-four-hour surveillance on that lock-up."

"For how long?"

"I'll let you know. Don't worry, I'll give you the budget. If there's movement, I want to be there. You get Barnes and I want Hamilton, but whatever happens, I don't want either of them interviewed or charged immediately. I want to talk to them first."

Wilcox said, "But I get Barnes?"

"If he has nothing to do with my current investigation, yes."

Chapter 26

Amanda jumped in a pool car and headed to Kensington to the offices of accountants Sharp and Stevens. The traffic was heavy and the drive took about twenty minutes. A well-polished brass plate suggested that the firm was still around, and she ascended two floors and walked into a small reception area. An efficient-looking receptionist smiled patronisingly and enquired how might she assist.

Amanda said, "I'd like to speak to Mr Sharp or Mr Stevens."

The receptionist looked unimpressed. "Yes, madam, which one of them do you have an appointment with?"

"Neither of them, "Amanda admitted.

The receptionist screwed up her face, and, studying her computer, said, "Normally an appointment is necessary; they are both very busy. I will see when they might become available."

There was a time for courtesy and patience, but it wasn't right now. Amanda flashed her warrant card and said, "This is urgent. I want to see both Mr Sharp and Mr Stevens now."

The receptionist held her patronising smile for an instant but it fell. She had the grace to know when she was beaten. "One moment, madam," she said and rose sharply and disappeared behind a door, eventually returning with a portly middle-aged man dressed in an accountant's uniform.

Stevens directed Amanda to his office. "Please have a seat, Miss Barratt."

Amanda said, "Is your partner available?"

"No, I'm afraid he is out of the office."

Amanda laid down the annual accounts of the Superior Catering Company and said, "I am conducting a confidential enquiry on behalf of the Home Office. This interview is subject to the provisions of the Official Secrets Act and I urgently need information about this company."

Stevens started confidently. "Yes, a very profitable company. We prepared the accounts for four or so years. Since they started, I think." Warming to the subject he went on, pointing out a page in one of the reports. "Very good margins, exceptional really and, of course, good cashflow – which is often a challenge in this type of business."

He took a deep breath, as if in preparation for a further exposition of the importance of cashflow in the catering trade, but Amanda interrupted him and said, "Tell me about the director."

"I met Mr Ross, but just a few times. He was well-spoken and well-educated. A good businessman. I think he was an accountant to trade, but either way a financial expert. He was really very sharp when it came to money."

Amanda asked, "Yet the firm was liquidated?"

"Yes, but a voluntary liquidation. I think because Ross became ill. He was really the driver and the brains behind the business. When he was unable to work it went downhill quite quickly."

"What was wrong with him?" Amanda asked.

Stevens said, "No idea."

"Strange that such a profitable business would just vanish."

"It happens, but, yes, it really was extremely successful. The profit margins were higher than I've ever seen."

"Why was that?"

"They catered to an expensive crowd. Ross seemed to be well-connected."

"What sort of people?"

"Highgate set, politicians, big businessmen, I think. I once asked Ross about it. He said that these sorts of people would pay anything."

"Well, they're usually using other people's money."

Stevens smiled.

Amanda asked, "And the business closed about a year ago?"

"About that. Maybe Ross just wanted to retire. He had made enough money."

"And you've heard nothing about Ross since?"

"Nothing."

Amanda left the office and returned to her badly parked squad car. She phoned Max.

"Give me a chance, boss."

"Yes, sorry, but I have a little more on David Ross." She told him.

"I'm way ahead of you, boss. Middlesex Cottage Hospice."

Chapter 27

Sheila Cahill was early for her latest appointment with Patrick Lawrence.

She showered and dressed quickly, then searched out the little attaché case and the buff folder that contained all her evidence. She moved into the drawing room and began to review her typed notes, then checked that two copies of the recording were in place – one on her desktop computer and the other on a memory stick. She tested them both. Both crystal clear. She replaced everything neatly in the case, lit a cigarette and ran through her plan again. It was flawless. Unsurprising: it was her plan.

The doorbell pealed. The pull of the hall mirror couldn't be avoided. Not bad. In he came, striding powerfully past her.

She fixed him a drink. He looked a little different today. Sitting higher in the chair, not clean shaven but a lot tidier. His clothes, still casual, had better labels and sat well on his powerful frame. Even his voice was different: the voice of an assertive professional man on an important assignment.

She handed him a drink and held his gaze pleasurably. Maybe a confident Lawrence might prove less pliable? No; however professional Patrick could be at his best, he would be no match for her. "Right, Patrick, let's make a start. It's time for you to see and hear the rest. Now, timing is crucial, and in return for this story, all the evidence and ongoing exclusive off-the-record access, I must insist that only I determine when and how we do this."

"It's your show," Lawrence said. "What's the timetable?"

"We should move fast. Confront Adam with our findings. We have an opportunity this weekend. Will that suit you?"

"Of course."

"Adam's got a villa in Malta. It's the only place he can go without staff or security. We'll catch up with him at the villa."

"Does he know we're coming?"

"No, I think we should surprise him."

"Will he be alone?"

"I'm sure he will be. It's the perfect setting away from prying eyes. When he sees what we've got, it shouldn't be too difficult to convince him to resign and, of course, discuss the transitional arrangements."

"I've been thinking about this. Why on earth would Chandler agree to help you to the leadership after you've destroyed him?"

"What choice does he have? This stuff puts him in jail. I'll spare him that. He can even keep his pension and reputation, if he helps me."

Lawrence said, "I want all of this story. Just me."

"Yes, of course, but remember: a bit at a time."

"But three or four years?"

She smiled, "Maybe not as long as that, and remember, I'll be in number 10. There'll be other scoops."

"What's to keep you from forcing Chandler out and killing the entire story? I mean, all I've got at the moment is your story."

"Surely you trust me."

"You know I do."

Cahill smiled. "There are many reasons – firstly, you know all the background, and secondly, you're going to be there at the meeting. Although some of this will be totally off the record, that is until we agree a version, you could turn nasty if I welch on you and come after me in your paper."

Lawrence said, "Maybe, but journalism's not what it used to be. I spend most of my time these days writing junk for our proprietor and his business friends. If you're in Number 10, you could kill the story. Maybe even put me in jail."

"Now why would I do that when we can be so useful for each other?"

Lawrence smiled thinly.

Cahill smiled back. "Now, after our meeting with Chandler, we fly back to London. You get your exclusive resignation story ready and we'll agree the public reasons this weekend. At the same time, you will run a number of stories about me being the natural successor. Chandler will already have discussed things with party grandees, with others backing me, expressions of support.

"Every day, I'll give you, only you, the exclusive line. With luck there'll be no contest, more of a coronation. Remember, I'll have all the main backers behind me. Chandler will see to that. We keep going in this way, and after I've won the next election, you can go with the full story, in the paper and, of course, the book and serialisation rights."

Lawrence said, "And if things don't go to plan?"

"Why wouldn't it?"

"I don't know, but I've still not seen enough proof."

"Each day's story will come with a box of papers and notes, originals which'll stand up anywhere. Besides, you will learn much more this weekend."

"What about the recording?"

"No, I'll keep that for the moment. Just be patient. Keep it for the book."

"It would be quite helpful to the public to see a blackguard and a crook jailed."

"Fuck the public. They'll get good government, what else do they want?"

Lawrence shrugged.

Cahill said, "Look, Patrick. It took Woodward and Bernstein to kick out a US president. You're going to do that all on your own."

"Can I at least hear the tape?"

Cahill sighed. "All right, but you can't get a copy. Not yet." She opened her attaché case, produced a memory stick and inserted it into her laptop.

Lawrence tensed. The computer came to life, clear as a bell. The exchange barely lasted a minute.

Sheila moved across, stopped the machine and replaced the memory stick in her attaché case. "Well, what do you think?"

"The smoking gun."

"Exactly."

Lawrence said, "It sounds like Chandler, sure, but can you be certain?"

"Yes of course, I've known Adam for years. That's him."

"Who's the other?"

"Not sure."

"Surely there's a record of attendees at Downing Street."

"Not all unofficial visits are recorded."

"Isn't the voice familiar to you?"

"Not to me," she admitted, "but I'm looking into it."

"Didn't you ask around?"

"Look, the tape's just the icing on the cake. We've got more than enough. Do you agree?"

"Yes, I think so. It's pretty conclusive."

Chapter 28

Amanda Barratt was an impatient woman, and although less than half an hour to locate a hospital patient in Greater London represented a decent effort, she repeatedly urged her driver to get her to the Middlesex Cottage Hospice. Was this ridiculous note at the heart of things?

David Ross had connections. Political connections, the accountant had said. Could he be in danger? Could he be involved? Who knew?

"How long now?"

"Five minutes, ma'am. A minute less than the last time you asked."

She deserved that, so she shut up for the rest of the journey.

The driver left half an inch of the tyre tread on the road when not quite overshooting the left turn into the leafy car park of the small single-storeyed hospice. Her colleagues were already there, which relaxed her a bit. After confirming that they had front and back coverage, she pushed open a sturdy glass entrance door and went inside.

A middle-aged grey-haired receptionist awaited.

Amanda said, "I'm here to see Mr David Ross."

"Yes, madam. If you will wait here, I will get Mrs Forrest."

The leader appeared. A tall spare woman of about fifty. She extended her hand. "I wonder if you might button up your jacket,

Miss Barratt. Our residents might not be ready for the sight of a Glock 17."

"Probably not," Amanda agreed. "You know guns, Mrs Forrest?"

"No, but I watch a lot of television thrillers."

"I'm looking for Mr David Ross."

"A long-term patient. He is sleeping. He sleeps most of the day, I'm afraid. Must you need to see him immediately?"

"Yes, and have a look around his room. I may have to leave some of my people here."

"Follow me."

After a couple of turns down narrow corridors, Mrs Forrest stopped and knocked gently.

No response.

She then slowly half-opened the door and slid inside. She re-emerged and beckoned Amanda inside. "Ten or fifteen minutes at the very most, Miss Barratt."

As Amanda entered, David Ross was still straining to sit up in his bed – a dark-haired and dark-eyed man of about fifty-five with a surprisingly robust frame for a man with such a depressing prognosis. He replaced a small brightly covered diary and a pen on the bedside table.

"Mrs Forrest says that you're a police officer."

"Well, sort of. I'm from the Home Office. Amanda Barratt."

His eyes brightened. "Home Office, that sounds important. Well, to what do I owe the pleasure?"

"Is it a pleasure?"

"Believe me, anything out of the ordinary is a pleasure. Every day, all twenty-four hours of it, rain, hail or shine, I spend in this bed. I'll get out of it when I die."

"How long have you been here?"

"A year tomorrow. I count the days. What else can one do?"

Sometimes this job was just rotten.

"I'm going to call you Amanda. Will you call me David?"

"Yes, of course."

"So why are you here, Amanda?"

Why was she here?

"I'm investigating a death, and in the victim's house, I found a flyer for the Superior Catering Company."

Ross screwed up his face quizzically. "Amanda Barratt of the Home Office comes to see me urgently because of a flyer of a defunct company?"

"I'm not a very experienced investigator."

Ross sat forward and looked at her through narrow eyes. "You know, I don't think I believe that, Amanda."

"The name of the deceased was John McMahon. He lived in Paddington."

"The name means nothing to me."

"Why would it? Mr McMahon was a man in reduced circumstances. A lonely man in the grip of a drug addiction."

"A sad story. What happened to him?"

"Someone broke into his bed-sit and snapped his neck."

"Nasty, but what can I tell you?"

"He had one of your flyers pinned on his wall."

"And?"

"Maybe a former customer of yours?"

"Could be, but I didn't know every one of our customers."

Amanda said, "I'm told you had a very profitable business and a lot of upmarket clients."

"I was lucky. I did well, but now I spend all day in bed. I mean, what use is money?"

Amanda parked this oft-asked question. "I'm chasing down another line. If I told you that the dead man was trying to blackmail the prime minister, what would you say?"

Ross looked puzzled. "Blackmail Adam?"

"Adam? Do you know Adam Chandler?"

"Of course I know Adam," said Ross. "We were at Oxford together. He was a friend and he still is. I was a bit sweet on him once, but he was never interested – just the reverse in fact: a bit too keen on girls. I told him often he ought to watch out for the tabloids. He visits me when he can. But what could Adam be blackmailed over?"

"Well, perhaps his fondness for women, as you put it?"

"Does anyone care about sex these days?"

"Seems it's just me," Amanda admitted. "When did you last see Mr Chandler?"

"About a month ago."

"He visits you regularly?"

"Yes, when time permits."

"That's considerate of him. It is so hard to really know someone from their public image."

"Very true," Ross agreed.

Amanda said, "Mr Chandler is also preoccupied with the deaths of Phillip Allardyce and Colin Patterson."

"I read about that."

"Did you know them?"

"I did a lot of political functions and dinner parties. I met Patterson a couple of times. Allardyce, I never met. I've heard of him. I used to follow politics quite closely."

"Who were your political customers?"

"All the movers and shakers at one time."

"What are your politics?"

Ross laughed, "None really. When you've seen politicians up close, it can put you off. Besides, they all pay well. Why alienate possible customers?"

"I often feel the same," Amanda admitted, "but I imagine you are a supporter of Mr Chandler?"

"Well, you could say that, but more personally than ideologically, to be honest."

Ross's eyelids fell a little.

"You're tired, Mr Ross. I think I've outstayed my fifteen minutes."

"Mrs Forrest is a stickler for the rules, but forget her. You are talking about three deaths here. One murder and two others … well, you didn't say. Were Allardyce or Patterson murdered as well?"

"I don't know," Amanda said.

"But you tell me the man, McMahon, was blackmailing Adam, and now he's dead. Are you saying that he might have been killed because he was blackmailing the prime minister?"

"I'm not saying anything at the moment."

Ross pursed his lips. "The Home Office has a lot of departments."

"Yes."

"So, what are you, Amanda?"

"I'm someone trying to make sense of the death of a man. That's all."

"Well, the suggestion that someone like McMahon being killed because of some lame blackmail attempt is fantastic."

"Everyone keeps telling me this … and then someone else dies."

"Are you expecting more deaths?"

"I don't know."

Ross had a thought. "Am I in any danger?"

"Why would you be? As you say, you know nothing."

"That's true. Besides, why kill a dying man?"

Amanda said, "Can I come and see you again, perhaps tomorrow?"

"Yes, of course, Amanda." Ross's voice was thin now, and he was slipping noticeably down in the bed. Although his eyes retained some of their earlier fire, suddenly he looked very tired.

"Okay, David, that will do me for now. I'll let you sleep."

His voice was barely audible now. "Good days and bad days, Amanda."

His eyes were shut now, but as Amanda rose to leave, Ross whispered her name, and with a slow movement of a thin, loose-skinned arm that seemed to be indescribably heavy, he beckoned her.

She moved near to him.

"Amanda, you might not believe this, but I've enjoyed meeting you. Love's all that matters. Find someone you can love and who loves you as well."

Amanda rested her hand on his brow as his eyes closed. She waited a moment until she confirmed some light breathing. And then (did she imagine it?) a suggestion of a tear on Ross's cheek. This was quite enough misery for one interview. She shut the door gently, deep in thought, and walked slowly back to the reception.

Mrs Forrest said, "Well, Miss Barratt. Did you get what you need?"

"No I didn't, but he's an interesting man."

"Yes. Very clever also."

"I will need to talk to him again. He became very tired."

Mrs Forrest said, "You were nearly twenty minutes. That's a very long time for Mr Ross. Was he coherent?"

"At first, although he seemed to drift off near the end."

"Is there anything else I can help you with, Miss Barratt?"

"Do you keep a record of visitors?"

"No, I'm afraid not. However, just a minute." She left and opened a glass door to an office. A moment later she returned. "Come through, Miss Barratt."

A plump middle-aged woman was sitting at a cluttered desk.

Mrs Forrest said, "Ann, can you help us? We're interested in any visitors that Mr Ross has had recently."

"None as far as I know. Maybe Fiona Lewis knows, but she's on holiday."

Amanda said, "Is she contactable?"

"Sorry, she's gone abroad."

"Back when?"

"Next week."

"Okay, thank you. Could we have a private word, Mrs Forrest?"

The plump middle-aged woman departed at a signal. Amanda said, "I'd like to leave one of my staff here. Just for a few days."

"Why would that be necessary?"

"I'm not really sure, to be honest. Just for a few days."

"Are we in danger?"

"I don't think so, but Mr Ross may have information that I need for an active enquiry."

The door opened behind Amanda and a slim woman not much more than twenty joined them.

Amanda said, "This is Emma, Emma Hutton. She works for me."

Mrs Forrest looked as if she had more questions but opted for efficiency. "Well, we have a spare desk at reception, and I can have a chair organised outside Mr Ross's room."

"Yes, that will do fine," Amanda said.

Chapter 29

These arrangements made, Amanda stood in the carpark reviewing her next move, but Inspector Wilcox's telephone call decided that for her. She jumped into the car and for the second time that day embarked on a hair-raising trip through the London traffic. The car screeched to a halt some way short of the ultimate destination, and they completed the journey to a nondescript flat on foot.

Inside, Inspector Wilcox and two plain clothes officers were jostling for space and sharing an expensive selection of optical aids. Through binoculars, Amanda viewed the activity at the lock-up. The scene was a simple one: three men engaged in the task of unloading the contents of a heavy goods vehicle.

"Do we know them?" Amanda asked.

"Yes, Jason Barnes is the blond heavy-built one, the other two work for him."

"When did the lorry arrive?"

"Ten minutes ago."

"Is Hamilton there?"

"There's someone in the lock-up," Wilcox said. "We think it's him, but we're not 100% sure."

"How long to empty the lorry?"

"They've been at it for about ten minutes, ma'am."

"Are you ready?" Amanda asked.

Wilcox conducted a couple of radio conversations. "Ready when you are, ma'am." He threw her some body armour. "Are you armed?"

"Yes."

The flat had been well-chosen, and via a back door they moved through a long narrow unkempt garden, which ended with a high stone wall punctuated by a badly maintained wooden door. It had only a few hardened strips of its original green paintwork remaining and the naked wood was heavily weathered.

Wilcox said, "We're exactly opposite the lorry. Be careful. Do you want me to try it?"

Amanda shook her head and slowly turned a rusting metal handle. It squealed a protest, and she stopped turning and looked at Wilcox. Silent deliberations were quickly abandoned. A barely audible noise was gathering. Metal on metal. She put her hand on Wilcox's arm and pointed upwards.

As the train thundered over the railway arches, Amanda turned the creaking handle and roughly opened the elderly door, with Wilcox and two supporting officers a step behind. They moved alongside and fanned out silently.

The men at the lorry had either finished or were on a short break. Now, they were only about ten yards away. All three were smoking and two had their backs to them. Only the blond man faced them, and he didn't react before Amanda crouched low and screamed out a warning.

Her voice carried, and then it was every man for himself. One man sprinted to the head of the alley and back towards the station, while another ran into the lock-up and slammed the door behind him.

The blond man didn't move. He looked at Amanda and she watched in slow motion as he laughed and pushed his leather jacket aside.

"Don't be silly, Jason."

He smiled again, and very slowly raised his hands behind his head. "You know, I'm going to take your advice. I've decided not to die today."

"Good decision, Mr Barnes."

She edged towards him, joined by a couple of policemen who cuffed Barnes.

Amanda looked down the alley. The running man was now on the ground face down, alive but under arrest. That just left the lock-up. Amanda and Wilcox stood one side of the door leaves against the brick archway, their two colleagues on the other side. She leant across and banged the butt of her pistol against the door. "Armed police. Come out with your hands on your head."

Again, this common-sense appeal paid off, and a voice from within cried, "Don't shoot, I'm coming."

Amanda withdrew, and a moment later the wicket gate clicked. It inched open. Guns were raised, but they were destined to go undischarged as a man, very tentatively, emerged with his hands reaching for the sky, all the time advising frantically that they should not shoot.

He lay on the ground without being asked and after some short, rough handling, Amanda said, "Is there anyone else in there?"

"Just the old man."

"Is he armed?"

"No."

Amanda decided to make use of the man on the ground. She kicked him persuasively to his ribs and shouted, "Get up."

With a scared face, he obeyed.

"Now get over to that door and slowly, very slowly, open it."

The man drew the door back slowly to reveal the scene within. Columns of boxes were crammed either side of the lock-up, except for one box, which was open.

Amanda holstered her gun and walked inside. She looked into the box. Interesting.

Alongside, Lord St John Hamilton sat with his head in his hands.

Chapter 30

It had been a long day and Amanda still had a lot to do. She needed to speak to Jason Barnes and Lord Hamilton, but they could wait a bit. Mostly she wanted to speak to David Ross again, but that would have to wait until he recovered some strength.

Fuck it. Everything would have to wait. She wanted to spend some time with someone who wasn't a criminal. She would go and see Jack and have a drink and some cigarettes. They could review the case together and maybe she would kiss him.

Jack Edwards was an annoying man. He wasn't all he could be, and he usually wasn't all that she wanted him to be. He had been on her mind more recently, and yesterday he said that maybe he loved her.

The concierge waved her through and she went up the stairs, pushed the bell and waited. The sound of music drifted into the corridor. It sounded like jazz. Odd. Jack only played jazz when he was in a good mood. The door opened. No doubt about it, he was happy.

He was shoeless and wore a pair of cords and a heavy cotton shirt which was at least half unbuttoned, freely displaying a small amount of chest hair, a common affliction in men over forty. He was unshaven and his dark hair was unkempt and a bit long, but the overall effect was, she conceded, pretty sexy. He looked at her and swallowed a piece of spaghetti he had been chewing. There were cooking smells from the kitchen. She kissed him on the cheek. "Oh good, dinner. I'm starving."

He smiled back. Nice, but not the usual smile. Miles Davis blasted on.

"What's up?"

"Oh nothing. I've got someone with me."

That was okay in theory but now, standing in his warm corridor with the music and the food smells, she didn't like it.

It would be a woman, of course. Straight men like Jack Edwards did not look like that in the presence of other men. As far as she knew, Jack didn't know any women in London – so who was she?

As far as she knew, she repeated. How far had she taken the trouble to find out? Not far, she acknowledged.

Maybe she had a rival? Oh well, fuck it.

"Can I come in?"

"Of course."

She threw her coat across a bench in the hallway and gathered herself to her full height, preparing for a power entrance. She was as tense and alert as if surprising an armed felon, but this readiness proved unnecessary as the lounge was unoccupied.

Jack followed her in. "Do you want a drink?"

"Yes, please."

She watched as he mixed it and brought to her. He did not mix one for himself, so presumably he already had one. She smiled sweetly and said, "So how did you get on today with Ray Dewar?"

"Oh, quite well. Actually, she's here now."

"A novel means of interrogation."

"I like to be thorough."

Amanda laughed but found herself wildly wondering if Jack had slept with her. Annoying. Maybe the upcoming meal, under candlelight no doubt, was part of a more traditional wooing attempt? Christ, maybe she was in his bed right now? She was on the point of admitting to herself that this would upset her when from the kitchen, a sexy, playful voice called out.

"Jack, Jack, where are you? Come through immediately and give me a hand."

A moment later the lady herself bounced in. She was casually dressed in jeans and a cotton shirt that hung loose not far short of her knees. It was big but it wasn't Jack's shirt. Her red hair was redder than Amanda remembered: short and thick and tousled, and, with her green eyes and pale, unmade-up skin, her overall appearance was impressive. She perched herself on the edge of the sofa. She was barefoot. She had no flaws, and was at least six years younger than Amanda, but Amanda was relaxed now. Although he didn't know it yet, Ray Dewar really wasn't Jack's type.

She didn't snub Amanda; it was just that she looked at and spoke to Jack first. "We're nearly ready through there. Now where will we eat – here or the dining room?"

Jack at last said, "Ray, this is Amanda."

"Oh, the lady from the bar. Nice to meet you again. Are you staying for something to eat?"

The casual assumption that issuing such an invitation was within her gift was irritating, but Amanda let this power play pass and flashed a complacent smile. "Yes, that's very kind, I've had a pretty tough day." Unlike the two of you, she thought.

Ray Dewar said, "Well, have a seat. I need to see to the food."

Jack also got up, but to Amanda's satisfaction, he didn't follow Dewar to the kitchen. He mixed himself a drink and took the seat opposite Amanda. He took a long mouthful of the drink and seemed unable to put his thoughts into words. As he struggled, she decided that the situation was far from a crisis, not even a drama. Maybe it would prove useful.

"Thanks, I'm starving. She seems nice."

"Yes," was all Jack could manage. Poor Jack.

Amanda said, "Look, you sit there, and I'll go and help."

Chapter 31

Jack poured himself another drink as Amanda headed into the kitchen. That had been a strange experience. Amanda jealous and him feeling guilty. Their relationship seemed to have moved on.

The food was good but the sit-down meal proved not to be the free-flowing nor intimate occasion it might have been with just two.

Dewar insisted on employing the never-used cavernous formal dining room – a room kitted out with an endless brightly polished mahogany table that sat about two dozen and, to Jack, represented the high watermark of his designer's folly and extravagance. He didn't have twenty-four friends – he doubted whether he knew twenty-four people – yet the flashily appointed room was here just in case.

Still, when you had two beautiful women in your flat looking after you, one was a little better than friendless and, he supposed, he shouldn't complain. As for the sitting arrangements, Amanda had put him at the head of the table while she and Dewar sat on his right and left hand, opposite each other. With an effort, Jack could just make out the other end of the table. Against the odds, Amanda and Ray Dewar seemed to get on well.

Throughout the meal he had glanced at one and then the other and, having with iron resolve determined not to compare them, spent the entire meal doing just that.

Amanda left the table momentarily. He poured Ray another glass of wine and said, "That was a great meal."

She smiled and admitted that it was her speciality. "What job does Amanda do? Is she your boss?"

Before he had answered, Amanda returned and, evidently having overheard the question, said, "I work for the Home Office."

Ray Dewar seemed impressed. "That sounds exciting."

Amanda demurred and told an easy lie. "No, not really. Mostly dogs fouling streets, traffic offences and meetings with residents' groups. Pretty mundane, really – well away from the sharp end."

Ray seemed disappointed, and with the openings for further questions gone, she said nothing.

Amanda reciprocated. "And what about you?"

Ray Dewar said, "I'm self-employed. A freelance researcher. Mostly I get commissions from TV producers and writers. Sometimes big companies – employee-screening activities, very occasionally political research. On one level, I suppose it's quite interesting, but on another level, it always means raking around the internet, the British Library and then writing a report."

"How did you get into that?" Amanda probed.

"I left university, had no idea what I wanted to do and came to London to take a year out. A friend who was writing a book on the history of English agriculture asked me to help. I did it and the friend had another friend and so it went on."

Amanda changed the subject quite abruptly. She said, with a hint of sharpness, "You interested in politics, Ray?"

Ray Dewar either didn't notice the tone or chose to ignore it, and her voice was still friendly. "A bit. Politics with a small "p" really, not really party politics." She explained, "I see, read and find out so much that one's bound to form an opinion and, as well, some of my commissions are from those looking to prove one side of an argument. It's not unknown for the research to be a little unbalanced. I mean, say you were researching for a TV programme on the inequities of the feudal system, then you naturally look for those inequities in your research. Most TV's political, at least to this extent."

It was a pretty reasonable answer, thought Jack, but Amanda persisted. "Yes, of course, I can see that, but what about you? Where do you stand on issues?"

Ray had picked up the tone now and reacted with measured asperity to this questioning. "What issues did you have in mind, Amanda?"

"Well, let's take the present government. Do you support it?"

"Generally, yes. I voted for them."

Jack said lightly, "Politics and religion, subjects that should never be discussed."

Amanda ignored this, and, still looking hard at Ray, said, "Have you ever worked for or done any research for a political party?"

Ray was being pushed into something nearing truculence now. "I can't remember."

Amanda leant forward aggressively and kept up the attack. "Come on, Ray. Try a bit harder."

Ray was openly annoyed now and decided that she had heard enough. She disengaged from Amanda's gaze and turned to Jack. "It's getting late. I should be going."

Ray was off the seat now, heading out, but was checked not by words from Jack, but by the firm grasp of Amanda's hand on her wrist.

Ray looked startled. Jack was bemused, and Amanda wore an expression of steely determination. "No, Miss Dewar. You're not going anywhere."

They hadn't even got to the coffee, but the little dinner party was over.

Ray recovered some spirit and shrugged off Amanda's clasp, saying, "Amanda, I will decide whether I go or stay." But she didn't move, and they all knew that despite these brave words, such a decision was no longer in her hands.

Amanda relaxed slightly and poured herself the last of the wine. "All right, Ray. It's time to make things a bit clearer." She delved into her top pocket and flashed her ID.

Ray eyed the wallet suspiciously and then picked it up, reviewed its contents and threw it back down on to the table.

Amanda retrieved her badge. "When we first met in the hotel, a man died, but I thought nothing of that. And then, last night, when I was investigating a murder, who should I spy but you, just around the corner from the scene. I'm an old-fashioned policewoman. I don't really believe in coincidences."

Dewar shrugged.

In a hard official voice, Amanda said, "Miss Dewar, I need to know all you know. I'm investigating three deaths. One murder, two others and a potential conspiracy in breach of the Official Secrets Act." This type of sledgehammer sometimes worked and it did tonight. Ray Dewar was white.

Amanda threw her a bone. "As far as I am concerned, you are guilty of nothing that I can see. Opposition research projects are common in politics. Not yet illegal."

"Opposition research. That's a loaded term."

"But you know all about that, Miss Dewar. It's all the rage in politics now. Gathering information on political opponents and using it for leverage when the time's right."

"I don't know much about that."

"Don't sell yourself short, Miss Dewar. It seems you're a bit of a legend in this field. Trip to the United States about ten years ago. Our American cousins are always so far ahead of us. Research, smears, media management. Quite impressive sometimes."

"But not so common in the UK."

"Quite common nowadays. The lifeblood of all of our young thrusting politicians."

"How do you know I've been in America?" Dewar asked.

"Don't be silly, Miss Dewar. In my own way I'm also a bit of a researcher. Not personally but as a director of MI5. I've got 5,000 researchers in Cheltenham and they've got a key for every door. What I'm interested in is your relationship with Sheila Cahill."

"She's commissioned a few things from me."

"No, a lot of things. In fact, she's your main client, and pretty much your only political client."

"I wouldn't say that."

"Your bank account says differently. You need to start telling me the truth. I haven't got time for any more shit. If it helps, I think your work is excellent. I particularly enjoyed your report on Adam Chandler and Alexis Patterson. A real bodice ripper."

"I don't remember that one."

Amanda said, "This is not a game, Miss Dewar. You may have important evidence or you may be involved in these deaths, so you and I will have to leave Jack here and have a further chat."

"How long will it take?" Dewar said sullenly.

Amanda didn't bother providing an estimate. The doorbell pealed, and she left and then returned with a couple of plain-clothes men who, in turn, left with Ray Dewar.

Jack was bewildered. "Are you going to tell me what the fuck that was all about?"

"Well, you heard it all."

"Did you know she was with me?"

"No, I'm not that good."

Jack poured himself a drink. "You want one?"

"No, I need to go."

Jack persisted. "Well, tell me more about Ray."

"Didn't you find out everything today?"

"Now that I think about it, I didn't find out very much."

"Did she tell you she met with Allardyce?"

"No. Did she meet with him?"

"I don't know. I'll ask her later. I was planning to pick her up tomorrow." She smiled at Jack. "But you picked her up first."

"Funny. What else do you know about her?"

"Just what you heard. No criminal record. From the west country." She gulped down the last of her coffee. "Okay, I'm going now. By the way, we picked up Hamilton today."

"Oh."

Amanda touched his arm and laughed, "Cheer up. Some of your work may yet prove useful. Do you want to come with me?"

"If you want."

She thought about it. "No, I'll do this alone. I need official surroundings, maybe without the jazz and wine."

With this, she turned. "I'll call you in the morning." She kissed him on the cheek and, having completely fouled up his evening, was gone.

Chapter 32

After some words with the duty officer, Amanda followed a man with a large bunch of keys downstairs to a dimly lit claustrophobic corridor, then to cell number three. It was home to a toilet, a basin, a bed and, on the bed, the crumpled figure of a man.

"Do you want me to stay, ma'am?"

"No, I'll be fine."

The man on the bed stirred and sat up to face her.

Lord St John Hamilton presented an ancient and crumpled face. He flicked at a few strands of thin grey hair and straightened his shirt. "Hello, Miss Barratt. Are you here to release me?"

"I suppose that depends on how much you can help me."

"That sounds rather cynical, Miss Barratt."

"Yes, it's a danger in my profession."

"Just like politics," Hamilton continued, "the amount of lying is on an industrial scale. It's exhausting."

"I know what you mean. Everyone lies to me."

"Well, they will do, Miss Barratt. You've got power."

"I think about that quite a lot," Amanda said.

Hamilton sat up a bit straighter. "You're very easy to like, Miss Barratt. That's a great tool for an interrogator, but very dangerous for me."

"Here's the current position. We've picked you up in the company of known drug dealers. I'm told that we've found a gun and a small quantity of drugs. My colleagues in the police are a bit disappointed, to be honest. I think they hoped that this would be the big one and they'd get Jason Barnes this time."

"No doubt, the police will think of something."

"Not on my watch," Amanda said.

Hamilton fiddled with his hands and his eyes bore into hers. "Dare I believe that?"

"That is entirely your decision, Lord Hamilton."

Hamilton started cautiously, "Okay, what are you really after? I can't believe it's Jason."

"Jason. Is he a friend of yours?"

"No, I hardly know him."

"So, the question is, why did we pick you up with him at his lock-up?"

"I wanted to meet with him."

Amanda delved into her pocket and produced a large buff envelope. "Is this yours?"

Hamilton looked inside. "Yes."

"Do you often carry twenty thousand pounds with you?"

"I had some overdue bills to pay."

"Any interrogator would find that hard to believe. An ordinary interrogator would just assume it was to buy drugs."

"And what do you believe?"

"The simplest solution is nearly always the right one."

Hamilton laughed. "I hate drugs."

"Often the best way to raise quick cash."

"Maybe."

"And you needed cash?"

"The aristocracy always need cash."

Amanda shook her head. "We need to move forward more quickly, Lord Hamilton. People have died and I want to know why. If that's all you can tell me, you can take your chances with the police. With guns and drugs and cash, they'll probably go for a conspiracy charge. Maybe you'll get off."

And what are you offering, Miss Barratt?"

"That depends on what you tell me. And so far, you've told me nothing."

"How can I? I don't know what side you're on."

"I sometimes wonder that myself."

"Are you trying to protect Chandler?"

Amanda's heart leapt a bit. At last, something interesting. "No, I'm investigating these deaths."

"Wherever it leads?"

"That's what I intend."

Hamilton said, "Taking my chance on a conspiracy charge might beat an apparent suicide in a prison cell."

"Not my style," Amanda said. "I want the truth."

Hamilton laughed. "You really are plausible. I'm finding myself wondering whether I can trust a director of MI5. I must be crazy."

"The newspapers say that you are."

"And you believe the newspapers?"

"Of course not, the security services write most of the stories."

There was a knock on the cell door and a policeman came in. "Two coffees, ma'am."

Amanda handed Hamilton a mug. He looked at it with disappointment. "No milk and sugar?"

"No, but what about this?"

Hamilton accepted a dash of brandy and began to drink enthusiastically.

"Another before I leave?"

"Yes please. Just wait a moment, Miss Barratt."

"I'm listening."

"The money was for Jason Barnes. Not for drugs but for information."

Amanda knew when to say nothing.

"I believed that he could tell me something about Adam Chandler. Something that could destroy him."

"Strong words for a political rival."

"I don't give a fuck about his politics, but I do care about my daughter."

Chapter 33

Jason Barnes had been in a police cell many times, and he looked at Amanda neutrally as she interrupted his peace.

"The lady with the gun."

"Hello, Jason. I'm Amanda."

"What do you want?"

"I'm here to help you, Mr Barnes."

"That sounds unlikely. Besides, why would I need help? Since when were the police interested in a delivery of batteries?"

"I'm told there was a gun in the lock-up and a small quantity of drugs."

"Small beer."

Amanda said, "Maybe five years for the gun."

Barnes laughed. "I've got a licence for that shotgun. Wilcox will be disappointed."

"Yes, he's sick," Amanda admitted.

"I bet he is."

"Anyway, Jason, I'm very busy. How about a shorter sentence?"

"How much shorter?"

"Tell me what I want and you'll be out by the weekend."

Barnes sat up a bit. "What do you want?"

"I want to know about a job a few years ago. A shipment of cocaine. A big one."

"I don't know anything about drugs. I'm a businessman."

"We both know that's not true, but it can be for the purposes of this conversation. All I want is the information that Hamilton wanted, all of it."

Barnes shook his head.

Amanda leant forward in her seat and put her face very close to Barnes. "Last chance, Jason."

Barnes looked at her. "You're a brave girl."

"It's you who's brave, Jason."

"How's that?"

"Because if you don't help me, I'll run you and your miserable operation off the street."

Barnes laughed. "A war on drugs? It's been tried before."

"I haven't got time for that, but I have got time for a war with you. Just think of my options."

Barnes leant back.

"Full-time surveillance, unexplained wealth investigations, or then again I could leave you alone. Leave folks wondering how come Jason always gets away with it. Maybe your name will come up in the next drug bust. Being an informer can be fatal in your business, Jason."

"Have you any idea how often the police have said things like that?"

"Not really, but I'm not the police."

"No, you're the sort that comes when the aristocracy's in trouble. Is that what this is really about?"

"Not this time. It's simple. Tell me what Hamilton wanted and you're out and clear."

Barnes asked the usual question. "You think I can believe that?"

Amanda went into her jacket pocket. "Read this."

Barnes read it, shrugged and looked at her.

Amanda took it back and signed it with a flourish. "Here you are. I've sent a copy of this to your lawyer."

Barnes said, "You're releasing me before I tell you anything."

"Why not?"

"Well, I might leave and decide to say nothing."

"You might, but we've already discussed this. If you do that, you'll be seeing a lot of me and my department."

Barnes gave her his best smile. "Maybe I'd like to see a bit more of you."

Amanda smiled back and shook her head. "Careful what you wish for, Mr Barnes."

Barnes's lips tightened. The foreplay was over. He leant back on the cell wall. "Have you got cigarettes?"

She gave him one.

"All right, Miss Barratt. Hamilton has a crazy notion that Adam Chandler's somehow involved in drug smuggling."

"Why would he think that?"

Barnes shrugged. "They say the aristocracy are all mad."

"Is Hamilton crazy?"

"He's a believer in conspiracies."

"So am I. What particular conspiracy does Hamilton believe in?"

"He believes that Chandler is compromised and that he does favours for bad people."

"Compromised in what way?"

"I don't know."

"What sort of favours does he do?"

"I only heard of one, but it's probably another urban myth."

"I'm listening."

"They say that he helped facilitate a major drug shipment."

"Facilitate how?"

"It's an urban myth."

"Yet, Lord Hamilton was prepared to pay twenty thousand for this information."

"A fool and his money."

"When was this mythical shipment?"

"About eighteen months ago."

"Cocaine?"

"That's what I heard, but come on, your people know all about these things."

Amanda corrected him. "We know about most of these things, but as for the flood of cocaine last year, not so much. Just humour me. According to this urban myth, how is Chandler involved?"

Barnes said airily, "You know the sort of thing. Got the right people to arrange things and others to turn a blind eye."

"Hard to imagine that Chandler has the ability to arrange something like this."

Barnes laughed. "Of course he doesn't have the ability. He's a fucking idiot. But he has friends. Don't tell me you voted for him?"

Amanda said, "I don't vote."

"Well, why should you? It hardly matters. You guys run the country anyway."

"Why would Chandler do this?"

"For money, because someone has something on him. Who knows?"

Amanda said, "Twenty thousand seems a lot for so little information."

"That depends on how desperate you are to hear something that confirms your beliefs."

Very true, Amanda thought. "And Hamilton was desperate?"

"Twenty thousand pounds desperate."

Chapter 34

Ray Dewar didn't look as sexy as she had when barefoot in Jack's kitchen. She had been crying and, despite herself, Amanda felt sorry for her. Had she been heavy-handed? She reached across and put her hand on top of Dewar's. "Sorry about this."

Dewar scowled and half withdrew her hand.

"We don't need to do this here. If you'd prefer, I can take you home."

Dewar brightened and looked at Amanda. "Yes."

"Okay, come on."

Amanda led Dewar back to the reception and secured a car and driver. Dewar said, "Are you in charge here?"

"Let's say you are here at my discretion."

Dewar's Paddington flat, although in the same parade as the luckless John McMahon's, was a lot better. It had two bedrooms and the communal stairwell didn't smell. Dewar opened the door. Amanda sent her driver in first. In less than a minute he emerged. "All clear, ma'am. Do you want me to stay?"

"No, wait outside for me."

Whatever else Ray Dewar was, she was someone dedicated to work. The entire living space in the small apartment looked like a solicitor's office with bundles of files in every available space. The large working desk had two desktop computers and what looked like a couple of tablets.

Dewar removed a mountain of files from what was revealed as a small sofa and opted for her working seat at the table.

Amanda didn't need to prompt her and Dewar seemed to know what she had to do, riffling through files and papers. Eventually she turned to Amanda. "This is all I've got."

She handed over a bulging file.

"That's a lot of research."

Dewar shrugged.

"Let's just talk for a bit. Where are you from, Miss Dewar?"

"I thought you knew everything?"

"Not everything."

"Newcastle originally, but I moved to Wiltshire at a very young age."

"Where?"

"Just outside Swindon."

"Did your parents move job?"

A benign question asked blandly, but this one seemed to hit home. "My parents died very young. I lived with my grandparents." Dewar tensed, but Amanda carried on.

"An accident?"

"Something like that. My father was killed at work, my mother died a year later."

"Of what?"

"I don't think she recovered from his death, but I don't really know. I was very young at the time."

This was strangely interesting, but Amanda moved on. "I want to know about Sheila Cahill's project."

"She said it was research for a book."

"On what?"

"On Adam Chandler."

"When did you start?"

"About a month ago."

"A month ago," Amanda repeated slowly. "Did Sheila Cahill mention a note?"

"What sort of note?"

"A short crude note received at party headquarters, accusing Chandler of inappropriate behaviour."

"No."

"Presumably, like so many of your researches, Miss Cahill's requirements were one-sided. I mean, she was looking for the highlights – the best bits of the prime minister's life."

Dewar considered for a moment. "You would think so, but to be honest, I got the feeling she was looking for quite the reverse."

"That is interesting," Amanda admitted. "Did you find out anything that was critical of the prime minister?"

"Not much at first. A couple of folks described him as slick, that sort of thing, but really there was just the affair with Alexis Patterson."

"Did you meet Colin Patterson?"

"No."

"Never, not after hours?"

"No. I didn't meet him. I did phone him but he hung up on me."

"And neither of you mentioned his wife?"

"No, of course not."

Amanda said, "Why would Sheila Cahill be researching Adam Chandler? I thought they were close. A famous double act."

Dewar didn't laugh. "No one's close in politics. I've learned that much."

"Yet you accepted the idea of research for a book?"

Dewar tightened her lips. "At first I did, but really I think it was just cover."

"Cover for what?"

"Getting leverage on Chandler."

"Is she making progress?"

"Yes."

"Are there many sexual relapses?" Amanda asked.

"Yes, but no one's interested in sex these days."

"How many times am I going to be told this?" Amanda mused. "So, there's more."

"Yes, a lot more. It's all in that file."

"What about Mr Allardyce: were you at the hotel to interview him?"

"No, not interview exactly."

"What exactly?"

"Sheila asked me to find out who he was meeting."

"And did you find out?"

"Well, I got a photograph of you and Jack sitting with him in the restaurant."

"And you sent that to Miss Cahill?"

"Yes."

"What did she say?"

"Nothing."

"And you left the hotel soon afterwards?"

"Yes, I told Jack this."

"You didn't meet with Allardyce?"

Dewar hesitated.

"One chance, Miss Dewar."

"I met him briefly, just for a few minutes."

"And you talked about what?"

"The meeting that he had with you."

"What did Mr Allardyce say?"

"Just that you would be investigating."

"Nothing else?"

"He said that you didn't seem that interested."

Amanda said, "Now why would Mr Allardyce agree to meet with you and tell you these things?"

"He knew I was working for Shelia Cahill."

"And that you would pass on that message?"

"Yes."

"You told me you didn't know about the note?"

"I didn't know. Not at first. Not until then."

"And after this short meeting?"

"I left the hotel and drove back to London."

"And Mr Allardyce?"

"No idea. I left him at the hotel."

"Alone?"

"Yes, alone."

"Did he say he was meeting anyone else?"

"No."

"Did you see anyone else in the hotel you knew?"

"No."

Amanda opened the file in front of her and flicked through a few pages, mostly names of women and men connected to Chandler. Like everyone else no longer interested in sexual scandals, she turned the pages quickly. There it was. She felt sick. "John McMahon's on this list."

"Yes, I have spoken to him."

"Who gave you that name?"

"Allardyce."

"How did he know McMahon?"

"He saw him drop the note and followed him out into the street."

"And spoke to him?"

"I think so."

"And?"

"Nothing. He got his phone number and slipped him some money."

"Did he call him?"

"No. He gave me the number. I called him."

"Where did you meet him?"

"In a burger bar near Paddington Station."

"Not at his home?"

"No, I don't know where that is."

Amanda looked at her closely. "What did he tell you?"

"Stories about crazy sexual exploits, all at university. He didn't really have details. He wasn't all that sober."

Amanda said, "You do know that John McMahon is dead?"

Dewar's eyes widened. Her voice was shrill. "No, why would I know that?"

"Because he died in a fire. In a bedsit just a few blocks from where you live."

"I heard about the fire."

Amanda's voice was harsh. "Come on, you must have known him."

"No, no! I knew about the fire. Everyone did around here. That's all."

"Tell me again what Mr McMahon told you."

"Is this really necessary?"

"Yes, it fucking is. Just answer my questions."

"He really hated Chandler. He went on and on about how he was not fit to be prime minister. Mostly on the basis of his active sex life."

"Did he give a detailed account?"

"No, he just went on about affair after affair, mostly from years ago, and he suggested a few that were still going on. He gave a few names. Some of them are in that folder."

"Did McMahon tell you how he knew Chandler?"

"I don't think he did know him."

Amanda had an idea. A horrible idea. She flicked forward more pages. There it was. "And David Ross?"

Dewar's face whitened.

"Did McMahon give you that name?"

"Yes, he said that he used to work with Ross, and that Ross knew Chandler."

"Did you meet him?"

"Mr Ross was very ill. I interviewed him in a hospice, somewhere in Middlesex, I've forgotten the name."

"When?"

"Three weeks ago, maybe. Not long after Mr McMahon."

"What did you learn?"

"He told me nothing. It was a very short interview. I've told you – he was ill."

Amanda said, "Did you tell Sheila Cahill about Mr Ross?"

Dewar's eyes dropped. Her hand shook.

Amanda waited. It was one of those moments in an investigation when you knew you were about to learn something that took you miles forward but was just fucking horrible.

Dewar reached back to her desk and picked up a notebook. A cheap thing, but a notebook Amanda had seen before.

Dewar handed it to her.

Amanda scanned it quickly. Neat, familiar handwriting and impeccable grammar. Each transaction recorded and supported with succinct unambiguous narrative.

"How did you get this?"

"I took it. David Ross had it on his bed when I visited, and he just fell asleep, so I had a look at it."

"And?"

"I borrowed it. I thought I would copy it and then return it, but I couldn't get back to see him."

Amanda scanned a few more pages. "And did you discuss this with Miss Cahill?"

"Yes. I copied everything."

Amanda stretched both arms behind her head. "So, you know the contents of this booklet in detail."

It wasn't a question but Amanda got an answer of sorts. It was always the same when someone lost control. Shaking and every feature distorted. Terror. An attempt to speak didn't work.

"What is Miss Cahill proposing to do with this information?"

"What does that mean?"

"What does one ever use leverage for? To force resignations, get favours, gain power, sometimes money."

"I don't ask about that. I'm just a researcher."

Amanda said, "Give me your phone."

"It's in the desk."

"Hurry up."

She handed it to Amanda, who made a phone call with her own phone. "I'm going to check everything on this phone. Everything – and it better check out. Now you have to come with me. This is going to be a long night."

Chapter 35

Amanda's heart was racing, and her head was buzzing with ideas. She needed to think, she needed a drink, and she wanted to see Jack, but that would have to wait.

With Ray Dewar secured in the back seat, the Mercedes powered its way through the London traffic. She slowly shut her eyes and slipped back in the seat. Rest, relax. She couldn't.

Now she was fiddling with her Glock.

Once or twice, Ray Dewar knocked on the screen, but Amanda ignored it.

The Middlesex Cottage Hospice was peaceful enough as they sped into the lightly used car park. There was a dull outside spotlight illuminating the front door and most of the rooms looked to be dark.

The outer door was unlocked and Amanda passed the reception. Behind the glass sat a middle-aged woman in what looked like standard nursing fatigues, looking at her phone.

She would deal with this security lapse later, Amanda decided and, with her hand in her pocket and on the Glock, she jogged along the long narrow corridor, past silent doors, the bland carpet deadening her footsteps. She paused at the end of the corridor.

The gun was fully out now. A last corner. The lighting hadn't failed but was on the way out. When it flickered off the darkness was absolute, when on not much better – but good enough when you knew what you were looking for.

One of the things Amanda hated about being a professional was that it denied you hope. You couldn't, even for a second, pretend that Emma was still alive. Her body was still warm and her face looked untroubled. It wasn't clear how she had been killed, but there wasn't time for that. Amanda stood up and hurried towards the door to David Ross's room, which was very slightly ajar, with no light from inside. The book said she should wait on back-up, but she didn't have the book with her.

She took half a pace back and then crashed her boot into the flimsy door. It crashed off the wall, complained a bit and then gave up one of its hinges. She flicked on a wall switch and light flooded the room, still an attractive room and mostly in perfect order except for the door – and the pillow which sat on top of and not under the head of David Ross.

She pushed the pillow aside. Everyone looked different in life, but not when they were dead, with the features reverting to neutrality. She touched the neck. Dead but not cold.

She holstered her gun: a stupid move when she hadn't checked the room. And then a vice-like pressure on her neck. A slender arm but rock solid. There was no time to think, but thinking didn't matter now, only what was stored in your body and your sub-conscious. You against another. One of seven billion with unknown levels of strength, training and experience. She hadn't moved the slender arm an inch when another arm slithered and began to wrap round her head, a deathly serpentine movement. Somehow, she pushed it off, and either her flying elbow or her backward kick, which felt like it might have shattered a shin, dislodged the arm from her neck. Now she had a chance. She turned.

Her assailant, dressed in regulation assassin black with a regulation balaclava, wasn't all that much bigger than she. But now Amanda was favourite. A flash from the past came to her. Training at Catterick with the Parachute regiment. Throwing up and wanting to cry but getting through. The first female to pass the basic training.

Now things were slower. She was first to the punch, and a perfect, single piston-like straight drive to the point of the nose with the butt of her hand finished things. Amanda knew she had just killed someone. You always knew.

The figure just stopped, suspended in the air, then with no support slid, slowly and peacefully, down the wall to the ground.

Amanda's hand stung unbearably. She was alive. She leant over and removed the balaclava. She roughly investigated all the pockets. A break at last.

From outside, running footsteps and then, a scream. The Glock was out again. Leaning over the body of Emma, the nurse from reception looked up at her.

More of Amanda's experience kicked in now. The nurse was seconds away from a hysterical reaction. Amanda had no time for sympathy. She roughly took the nurse's arm and led her back to the reception, babbling vague and inadequate words of comfort and explanation.

She pushed the nurse into the office, shut the door firmly, and, laying her Glock on the reception desk, got on with her business.

It wasn't a long wait. Cars in the car park and then bodies, many bodies, coming through the door. She issued a few words of direction and they made their way along the corridor. Now she was tired, exhausted. She laid her head on the reception desk and enjoyed a short moment of escape from the madness.

"Do we really need to have a firearm sitting on our reception desk, Miss Barratt?"

Mrs Forrest.

"No, we don't," Amanda admitted and holstered the gun. "Why are you here?"

"I am the manager. My nurse" – she indicated the woman in the office – "called me."

Amanda opened her mouth to speak, but she was too tired to command.

Mrs Forrest said, "This is a small hospice, Miss Barratt. We only have a dozen rooms, but it is fully booked with people, many of whom have very little hold on life and need a lot of attention. It's important that your people understand this."

Amanda thought about mentioning the three dead bodies down the hall, but what was the point? Mrs Forrest had a lot more experience of death than she had.

"Right, Miss Barratt, you look as if you need a cup of tea."

Amanda followed Mrs Forrest pliantly into the office and accepted the drink. Sweet tea, the universal British treatment. It seemed to work.

Mrs Forrest busied herself by comforting her nurse, while Amanda took a phone call that she didn't want. She hung up and looked at the phone. "Fuck off."

Mrs Forrest looked round and delivered a silent rebuke before continuing whatever business she was engaged upon, opening and closing drawers, all the time tutting. "Ah, there it is," she exclaimed, clutching a small notebook. She placed it in front of Amanda. "I was asked to give you this."

Amanda opened the notebook. Interesting – and familiar.

Mrs Forrest handed her an envelope. "There's a letter also."

Amanda read it quickly.

"Is it useful?" Mrs Forrest asked.

"Yes."

"I thought it would be. So did Mr Ross."

Chapter 36

Jack was trying to sleep, but he wasn't having much luck, and he was forced to give up completely when the doorbell rang loudly.

Through the spyglass, Amanda looked confident and relaxed, but when he opened the door, her dark eyes were surrounded by black shadows. If it hadn't been Amanda, he would have suspected that she had been crying.

She passed him without a word, strode into the lounge and went straight to the drinks. "Do you want one?"

"No."

He sat down on a sofa and waited, while she took a long mouthful of whisky, topped up the drink and looked across at him. She made to speak but decided against it, instead throwing off her jacket, then making her way over to the couch beside him. She took another mouthful of whisky, put the drink on the table and leant back with her head against his chest.

Jack got ready to listen.

"I lost an agent tonight. Emma Hutton. She was just twenty-two. And it was my fault."

What could you say to that?

She reached across for her whisky, gulped down the whole drink, and returned to the sofa, shuffling closer into him.

"I left her at a hospice guarding a man – David Ross. Someone snapped her neck."

Jack had heard this sort of thing a few times, but it didn't feel any easier. He was grateful for that. Feeling sick to your stomach was how you should feel. "Who's Ross?"

"A terminally ill businessman."

"Did he have something to do with that fucking note?"

"Not directly, but he knew Chandler, and John McMahon used to work for him. I'm pretty sure McMahon just picked up a bit of idle chat."

"And that's what the note was about?"

"That's what I think."

"Maybe Ross was behind the note?"

"No, I don't think so. He was a nice guy."

"Was? Is Ross dead also?"

"Yes, he's fucking dead."

"Murdered?"

"Yes."

"Do you know why?"

"Nearly, I'm getting there. Ross left something for me."

"What?"

"A couple of detailed notebooks and a deathbed confession of a sort."

"A confession to what?"

"To things he did for Chandler."

"And these things were?"

"Managing his money."

"A financial advisor?"

Amanda laughed. "Not in the sense you mean. I haven't read everything yet, but it seems pretty simple. Chandler does favours for money, and the payment goes to one of Ross's businesses."

"Like the Superior Catering Company?"

"Yes, it's very simple. Buy about ten thousand pounds' worth of outside catering and pay a hundred thousand pounds. Over the odds, but so what?"

"A variation of the foundation racket. Half a million pounds for speeches after leaving office."

"Yes, something like that. Ross left me a lot of details. I need to read through it all thoroughly."

"Have you got the books with you?"

"No, I left them at the office. I've got folks poring over them now. As far as I can see, the notebooks are both the same. Your pal Ray Dewar had one of them."

"Sorry, I'm lost."

Amanda said, "Mr Ross was a clever man. He did everything in duplicate. That would be my guess."

"So that's the end of Chandler, and that's a good thing. I knew he was just another grifter. This will give you the chance to replace him with, well, another grifter."

"Hmm," Amanda said.

"What does that mean?"

"It means, don't get too excited. Things are complicated."

"You're not going to cover this up, surely?"

"We're not finished yet." Her voice seemed a long way away now. "I killed someone tonight."

This was promising to be a long night. Jack said, "Do you want another drink?"

"No, I'm too tired."

He was cradling her head gently now. It might have been vaguely romantic under other circumstances. "It's not your fault," he said weakly.

"Well, I don't agree, but thanks for that." She turned her face to him. "Sorry. I'm just venting. I'm meant to be the professional here."

"It's what I'm for."

She turned and kissed him on the cheek.

Jack said, "You must be exhausted."

"Yes, I am."

"Tomorrow's Saturday," he said hopefully.

She laughed. "We've got until six, that's when we're meeting Max at my office."

"We?"

"Well, you don't have to come."

"Of course I'll come. Now what about some sleep?"

Amanda yawned. "Can I stay here?"

"Of course," Jack said, harbouring a few illicit thoughts about the sleeping arrangements. He remembered his manners. "All the rooms are made up. Help yourself."

She lifted herself off him, got to her feet and extended her hand to help him off the sofa. She headed out of the lounge, holding his hand even tighter. At his bedroom, she led him in and said, "Can I sleep in here, with you?"

Jack's heart was pounding now.

"Just sleep, but I could use a cuddle."

A bit of him was relieved. He was a man and casual sex was meant to be something he should welcome, but that's not how he felt. His feelings for her were beyond that now.

She didn't flick on the light but threw off most of her clothes and jumped into the bed. He partially disrobed and gingerly got into the bed from the other side, maintaining a respectable distance. She turned her back to him and pushed herself against him. He put his arms round her waist and everything was comfortable.

She sighed happily.

He considered his next move and came up with a few options, but whatever it would have been, it was delayed forever by the sound of Amanda snoring lightly. In less than a minute, Jack was snoring too.

Chapter 37

Jack yawned. "When will Harris be here?"

Amanda yawned in sympathy and looked at her watch. "A few minutes."

Harris wasn't yawning and wore a broad smile. He looked as if he welcomed the interruption to his Saturday. "Morning, boss, hello, Jack."

Amanda said, "I've got a little work for you."

"Is it straightforward?"

"I don't know," Amanda admitted, "and it's a secret – you haven't been here."

Harris snorted. "As always, boss. What do you want?"

Amanda indicated the laptop on her desk.

"Whose is it?" Harris asked.

"A journalist, Ray Dewar."

"Never heard of her."

"She's a freelance. She sometimes works for Sheila Cahill."

"Oh, I've heard of Cahill. She lies for the government."

"That's the one."

"Why are we interested in Dewar?"

Amanda leant back in her seat and looked at him closely. "I'm investigating the deaths of five people: Phillip Allardyce, Colin Patterson, John McMahon and David Ross." She paused.

"And the fifth?"

"Max, I'm sorry. Emma was killed last night."

For once Harris didn't have a glib reply. His eyes fell, and his voice was harsh. "What happened?"

"She was providing close protection for David Ross, the guy at the cottage hospital. They were both killed."

"Who by?"

"Someone who was after Ross."

"Who?"

"I'm looking into that."

"I want to help," Max said.

"Yes, but be patient. I'm waiting on forensic and other reports on the killer."

"The killer's dead?"

"Yes, I killed her."

"A woman?"

"Yes."

Max breathed in hard. "Okay, hand me the laptop."

Virtuosity in any field was always compelling. After a few seconds, Harris said, "Nothing on Colin Patterson, nothing on McMahon, nothing on Ross or Allardyce. What else do you want me to try?"

Amanda said, "Try Sheila Cahill."

Max got back to work. "A few emails from Cahill, talking about some report or a book. Doesn't say what it's about."

"Can you find the report?"

"Hang on. I need to get into this protected folder."

"Can you do that?"

"Obviously. There's a lot of files here."

"Print them all out."

"Give me fifteen minutes," Harris said, and disappeared out of the office.

Amanda leant back in her chair. "I can hardly keep my eyes open. Make me a coffee?"

Jack raised himself heavily from his seat and put on the kettle. "Was Max close to Emma?"

"Yes, very."

"Were they lovers?"

"No, nothing like that. Max is a very private person. A bit socially awkward really. Emma and he started working for me at the same time, the same day actually. She was about the only person he really talked to."

"He always seems so confident to me."

"You only see him when he's doing IT work. He loves it. It's an unhealthy obsession, but it's good for me. Outside IT, he's very shy, not confident at all."

The kettle boiled and Jack made coffee. Further discussion was deferred as Max returned with a bundle of papers, which he dumped on her desk.

Amanda began to leaf through the papers.

"Anything interesting?" Jack asked.

"Not really. Just the sort of thing that Ray Dewar told me about, but we need to go through these papers in detail. Max, can you check on Alexis Patterson?"

"There's something here. Do you want that printed?"

"Yes please."

Jack said, "Will that be about her and Chandler?"

"Probably."

"I meant to ask. How did you find out about them?"

"A detective needs good sources."

"GCHQ?"

"Don't be silly. The Whitehall car pool. These drivers know everything, and I know all of them. Chandler meets up with her most weeks. Usually short visits."

Jack yawned. "Well, I still say it's unimportant. When will you realise that no one's interested in the sex life of politicians these days? Don't you and the blackmail note writer understand this?"

"It seems I don't understand anything about this case."

Amanda's desk phone rang. A one-sided conversation.

"Problem?" Jack said.

"Not really, but annoying. It seems that Chandler left very early this morning for Malta."

"On his own?"

"Yes."

"Why Malta?"

"He's got a villa there. Had it for years. Uses it for weekend breaks. He goes there whenever he gets the chance."

"On his own," Jack repeated. "How can a prime minister do that?"

"Well, it's a bit irregular, but he's been doing it for years, and since becoming PM he's continued to do it. He absolutely insisted on privacy and he got his way."

Jack said, "Doesn't he take security with him?"

"No."

"Well, you'll have to forget about him until Monday. What about Cahill?"

Amanda frowned again.

Max returned. "Here's your report on Alexis Patterson."

Amanda scanned the two sheets and threw them down. "Nothing new." She looked at Max. "What I'd really like is to get in about Sheila Cahill's computer. Can you do that?"

Max hesitated. "Yes, I can, her emails on Ray Dewar's laptop don't come from a government machine. I could get into it if you're sure you want to."

Amanda said, "Is it difficult?"

"Not technically, but if you want me to do it now, it is a risk. I mean she might be using the machine."

As Jack was musing over the limits of power, Amanda looked across at him. "Well, should we do it?"

"You want my opinion?"

"Yes."

"It's possibly justified in this case, but as a general principle, I'm against this sort of thing. However, we were happy enough to hack

Ray Dewar's computer. Surely it can't be one rule for her and another for someone powerful?"

"Ray Dewar's a person of interest."

"Where is she, by the way?" Jack said.

"Safe."

"And how come you have her laptop?"

"I needed it."

"Well, that's fine then."

Amanda said, "How about making a decision? Should we hack Cahill?"

Jack hesitated.

"Come on."

"Well, perhaps after five deaths, getting into her computer is justified."

Amanda said, "Okay, Max, do it quickly."

Harris had already started. "John Lewis, Amazon, buys a lot of make-up." Another lightning series of keystrokes. "Podcasts, mostly political, boring stuff. Do you want me to look for the names of these dead people?"

"Yes."

Harris did so, and again found nothing relating to McMahon, Patterson and Ross. He said, "Emails from Allardyce. A lot of them. Seems they were close."

Amanda leapt out of her seat and stood alongside Max for a few minutes before sitting down again."

Jack said, "Well?"

"It's as I expected. Allardyce was hand in glove with Cahill."

"So, when he said he was against investigating the note, he was acting for Cahill."

"That's how I read it."

"To cover things up?"

Amanda laughed. "Try again."

It took about a minute of silence, then Jack said, "She had the note and was already investigating?"

"That's what I think. Remember, the original was missing. And when we met Cahill, she barely looked at the note and didn't ask for a copy. That struck me as unusual."

"And Ray Dewar?"

"She was researching for Cahill. She told you that last night."

Jack had a lot more questions but was interrupted by a loud intervention from Max.

"Something interesting, boss. Some kind of amateur audio recording. Do you want me to grab it?"

"Yes."

"I've sent it to your computer." He leant across. "Let me find it for you, save a bit of time."

Fifty seconds later they sat in silence. The quality was outstanding, and every word was clear.

Chandler's unmistakeable voice came first. "Hello, nice to see you again."

"You too, Adam," came back the response, "It's been a long time."

"Yes, what do you want?"

"Straight to the point as ever, Adam. I want five million pounds and some goods imported."

A pause. Then Chandler said, "I can't get that sort of money."

The other retorted in measured tones. "I know that you can."

"And what do I get?"

"Peace at last, Adam. It'll be over for ever – as if it never happened."

"How can I be sure that this is the last time?"

"You know you can trust me, Adam."

"Well, say I could raise that sort of money, when and how?"

"Very soon. I'll contact you. It must be done soon."

"Why now?" Chandler demanded.

"Because it's right for me now – I've had enough. I want out and this is my ticket. Do what I ask and be ready to do so soon."

Silence and then the other voice said, "Goodbye, Adam."

"Well that's a surprise," Jack said. "Another corrupt politician with a secret. Who's the other guy?"

"I don't know," Amanda said. "When was that recording, Max?"

"A couple of weeks ago."

Jack said, "The other man's Irish. Maybe it's McMahon?"

"No, McMahon's accent was much more southern Ireland, this is further north."

"How do you know that?"

"Don't you ever listen? I was born there, I can tell."

"Sorry, I forgot."

Amanda turned to Max.

"I can try, but it's a long shot." Max left the office.

Jack said, "Try what?"

"Don't you ever watch spy films?"

"Not often," Jack admitted.

"Voice recognition technology."

"Is there nothing you guys don't steal?"

"What do you mean?"

Jack lit a cigarette. "You started with fingerprints, then it was DNA, then faces, now voices. What next?"

"Whatever we need, I suppose," Amanda said wearily.

"How long have you been capturing voices?"

"Oh, quite a few years, but of course it really only took off with mobile phones."

"Is nothing safe?"

"Certainly not your phone," Amanda said.

"Depressing. Are voices unique like fingerprints and DNA?"

"I'm not certain. The technology is still maturing, but it can sometimes help. We have records of some of our more interesting targets. Just to set your mind at rest, we don't capture voices typically. However, I suppose when the technology is perfected, which it will be, who knows?"

"Oh, you will capture it, I'm sure of that."

"Maybe."

"Well, what are we going to do now?"
"Have a black coffee and a cigarette while I think."

Chapter 38

Jack might have been sleeping when Max Harris came back into the office. Well, it was seven on a Saturday morning.

Harris flopped on a chair and handed Amanda a sheet of paper, which she read carefully. "Frank Connor. How sure are you?"

"Not conclusive, but about an 85% acoustic pattern similarity. I assume you don't want to know about the cosine similarity and stuff like that."

"You're right. I don't."

"Who's Frank Connor?" Jack asked.

"A top man in Irish Republicanism."

"Is that still a thing?"

Amanda said, "It'll always be a thing, as you put it. But as for the sort of republican Connor is, well, they have been quiet recently, it's true."

"But I thought everything was calm these days."

"Well it's not making news headlines. Let's put it that way."

Jack said, "I've never heard of Frank Connor."

"Well, that's how he would want it. He's an impressive man."

"Impressive?"

"Well, maybe that's the wrong word, but he's been at the top of their organisation for years. He's ruthless and effective – and totally dedicated. He kills people."

"Have you had dealings with him?"

"No, but, interestingly, I met him once, about thirty years ago. He met my father at the house. I was just a girl. I came back from school early. I didn't know who he was at the time. My father told me years later."

Jack said, "Strange bedfellows."

"Not really. You'd be surprised how many so-called secret contacts there were between MI5 and paramilitary leaders in these days."

"But why?"

"Lots of reasons."

"Is Connor a spy, one of ours?"

Amanda laughed. "No, he is a totally dedicated republican. Lives like a monk, way out in the countryside, doesn't smoke or drink, and spends every waking hour thinking about his cause. And he's totally ruthless. They say he sanctioned the execution of his brother for informing. They call it touting, where I'm from."

"And you admire that?"

"No, but it gives you a guide to one's opponent."

Jack shook his head. "I don't understand any of this."

"It's because there are things you don't know."

"That's about the only thing I do know," Jack admitted. "How senior was your father?"

"He was the MI5 boss in Northern Ireland, although the command structure was complicated."

"Well, he should have just arrested Connor, if you ask me."

"And that would have solved things how?"

"Always the big picture."

"Usually," Amanda admitted.

Jack said, "But how would Chandler have dealings with Irish Republicans? All that stuff is way before his time."

"That's true."

"Are you doing anything over there at the moment?"

"Nothing special that I know of."

"Either way, Chandler's either involved with them or being blackmailed."

"Brilliant."

"So, you've got a pile of dead bodies and a corrupt prime minister now involved in something with a legendary terrorist. What now?"

"No one said it would be easy."

Jack laughed. "But seriously, what are your plans?"

"A bit of old-fashioned detective work, I think." She turned to Max. "Find out where Sheila Cahill is. I want to talk to her immediately. Pick her up and bring her here. No explanations, serious faces."

Max left and Amanda started fiddling with her mobile. "Here it is," she announced. She began to dial on her conference phone. After a couple a rings, a strong Irish voice answered.

"Hugh?"

"Aye. Who's this?"

"Amanda, Amanda Pierce."

A short pause. "Amanda. What a surprise. Good to hear from you. You'll be after a favour."

Amanda laughed. "What else?"

"Okay, let's hear it."

"Frank Connor."

"So, a big favour."

"A routine job, just a quick spot of surveillance. No problem to you. Do you keep in touch with Frank?"

"Not if I can help it, but I know where he hangs out. He's very quiet these days."

"Not completely, Hugh. He's been over here poking his nose in."

"Well, you can't keep a good man down. What do you need?"

"Just see if he's at home. If you find him, watch him for a day or so."

"Is it dangerous?"

"I don't think so, but dust off the Browning just in case."

"I take it this is unofficial."

"No, it's sort of official, just that it never happened."

"What rank are you now, Amanda?"

"Director."

"Well done you. Your old man would be proud."

"Not the way I'm handling this case right now."

"How do you want me to check in?"

She gave him a number. "It's scrambled, so no problem."

"When do I start?"

Amanda paused.

"I'm on it now. I'll be in touch."

Amanda ended the call.

"Amanda Pierce?" Jack asked.

"My maiden name. I haven't seen Hugh for years. He's retired now, but he was my father's top field man."

Max Harris returned. "Sorry, boss, I can't find Cahill. It seems that for the first time in living memory, she's off for the weekend."

"Where to?" Jack asked.

"Don't know. Her diary just says holiday, but hang on – she bought two airline tickets yesterday."

"To where?"

"Malta."

Chapter 39

Alexis Patterson was having a bad day, maybe her worst ever day. Her husband was dead, and her father was in a police cell facing prison and disgrace. Worse, her miserable bluff had failed, and Adam Chandler had stood her up.

He had promised to visit on Friday but had failed to show; nor had he called. Now it was Saturday morning and Alexis was half-dressed and sitting smoking in the kitchen over a cup of cold coffee. She waited and she waited, but still the phone did not ring.

She had put on a brave show with Adam at their last meeting, but it had been mostly bluff on her part. She knew that she could not keep him on any terms, not even terms which would make him despise her.

For the first time in her life, she felt powerless. Like all the other people. How did they live?

With a last flicker of energy, she wished revenge on him. Any sort of revenge. Furious base feelings invaded her brain. Thoughts she should never have, but once there they were tough to ignore.

"It was just sex, move on," she kept chanting to herself, but with each succeeding chant, it became a little more unbelievable. Without him, she knew she had nothing.

She stubbed out her cigarette, lit another and, pushing aside the cold coffee, reached for the bottle of cold whisky. When she was about halfway through it, she rose unsteadily to her feet. She halted for a moment and listened hard, but the phone was not ringing. It never would.

As she died inside, with a couple of stumbles she reached the bathroom. That was a mistake. The crisis might have passed, had she not caught sight of herself in the all-too-honest and ruthlessly efficient mirror.

Her face was blotchy and wrinkled and without the protection of make-up. The face of a woman on the edge of old age. A face that couldn't keep Adam, and if she could not keep Adam, then what else was there?

There was one thing left. It didn't seem that extreme now. It wouldn't get him back and it wouldn't hurt him, but maybe inconvenience him a little. It was all she had.

Fuck these safety razors. She drifted back to the kitchen. The oven wasn't gas-fired and the kitchen knives were blunt, but a bottle of a hundred aspirins was mostly untouched. She had very little experience of this sort of thing, but she did have about half a bottle of whisky left. She went to the kitchen and picked up a large wine glass and filled it. She threw a couple of the pills into her mouth and washed them down with a long draft of the cold whisky. This wasn't easy. She reached for the bottle of pills but it wasn't there, just a warm hand on her wrist. A vice-like grip.

"You don't need that, Lexi. I've sorted everything."

Chapter 40

Valetta Airport was a lot smaller than Heathrow and that was a good thing, as it meant that Jack did not have to endure twenty minutes of taxiing and manoeuvring before being released from the oppressive interior of the plane. Although he had been last to embark, he made sure he was first off and was soon relaxing on terra firma and enjoying the warm sunshine at the base of the portable steps, waiting for Amanda.

She was last off and led him away from the column of trippers to a reception area manned by a number of armed officials. They stood to the side as the officials made a cursory review of the incoming, and when the last of the tourists had been processed, one of the officials broke off from the main group and advanced towards them. He was tall and spoke in perfect English. "Miss Barratt?" He held out his hand. "Inspector Smith of the Maltese Police Force."

Amanda shook his outstretched hand and introduced Jack as Mr Edwards. Smith turned on his heel and led them past banks of officials and through the main concourse to a waiting car with a driver in place.

Smith again shook both of them by the hand, and after a few words with the driver, they moved off. They drove out of the airport, through some heavy traffic in a busy city centre, before halting outside the imposing wrought-iron gates of what proved to be the British High Commission. There were a range of flags flying outside the white mansion. Maybe the building was shared but, looking out across the bay, past massive yachts, it looked like a decent posting.

It proved more difficult to gain access to this little corner of England than it had been to enter the country, but after a number of phone calls, eventually a man, not out of his twenties, and, Jack speculated, straight out of Oxford or Cambridge, arrived. He introduced himself as Vice Consul Anderson and led them through the leafy grounds and through a spacious building to his colonial relic of an office.

He was succinct and gave the impression that he had better things to do on a Saturday. After a bland briefing on the geography of the island, he led them to another smaller and smoke-filled office, which was occupied by an untitled man introduced only as Barber.

Barber was about fifty, overweight and wasn't out of Oxford or Cambridge. He spoke with a thick Midlands accent in between drags of poisonous local cigarettes. "Well, Miss Barratt, what brings you out to Malta? A weekend break?"

"No, just a little business."

"So, what's this all about?"

"Oh, just a little protection work."

Barber said. "I thought that house was owned by …"

"Yes, we know who owns it."

"Say no more."

Amanda said, "How did you get on at the house?"

"There was hardly any time," Barber said, "but I managed to leave a couple of GSM devices, but only in the main lounge. I got a wall socket in as well. I chucked a calculator on the desk on the way out. It was pretty untidy so it should be okay."

"You weren't observed?"

"No, I was in and out in ten minutes."

"Good."

Barber handed Amanda a mobile phone. "Coverage is very good on that side of the island. Use this phone, the two numbers for the devices are stored on it. Anything else?"

"Yes, balaclavas and jackets, it gets cold at night."

Barber rose heavily and rummaged in a cupboard, then threw some clothing on his desk.

Amanda said, "Guns?"

"In the cupboard." Barber pointed.

"What have you got?"

Barber rose heavily and managed a few paces to a full-length cabinet which he threw open.

Amanda reviewed the armourer's store, and after picking up and examining several of the rifles, machine pistols and handguns, said, "Just the two Glocks."

Barber produced the guns and laid them on a table. A further rummage located boxes of ammunition.

Amanda handed a gun to Jack.

It was bigger and much heavier than he remembered. At moments like this he now knew for certain that the action sequences in movies were deeply flawed. He raised the gun in a mock show of competence. The barrel danced up and down, around and away from his imaginary target on the wall.

Barber looked alarmed but said nothing. However, Amanda seemed satisfied and took the gun from him, put the guns and ammunition in her holdall and said, "Where do I sign?"

Barber produced a sheet of paper, which Amanda signed. Barber returned it to the drawer without review and threw across some car keys.

Amanda said, "No, dropping us off would be better."

Barber scowled but, without comment, followed them outside and into a black Range Rover. Nothing was said during the thirty minutes or so that it took to get to the other side of the island, mostly lightly populated scrub land. They passed through a village. Amanda said to Barber, "How far away?"

"Less than half a mile."

"Okay, stop."

There was not another vehicle in sight. Amanda said to Barber, "Are all the arrangements in place?"

"Yes."

"Wait on my call. Keep close but out of sight of the house until you hear from me."

Barber grunted.

Jack and Amanda got out into the cooling evening and started to walk.

Chapter 41

It was after nine in the evening and about half an hour of daylight remained. Jack gazed out from his viewpoint behind a rocky limestone knoll. The ground was topographically complex, rough and uncomfortable, but Amanda had chosen a good position. To the left, endless yellow and brown scrubland leading back to the village, and to the right – dangerously near – were precipitous cliffs falling down to the azure blue ocean.

Off the main road, a small well-laid track, very near to the edge of the cliffs, led to the handsome white villa. It was a large, flat-roofed dwelling surrounded by a high wall, broken at the front by two iron security gates. Jack could see most of a courtyard, which lay to the side of the villa.

The footprint of the villa was very near to the cliff edge. From its rightmost side, there were a few steps which led to a flat, paved area, home to a table and surrounding chairs. The end of the patio was delimited, laughably, by a low chain railing posing as a health and safety feature. After that there was nothing, just blackness.

The patio allowed superb views over the Mediterranean, and through the little light remaining Jack noted the man on the patio taking in those views.

Jack handed the binoculars to Amanda. "Is that Chandler?"

"Yes."

"All on his own."

"It looks like it. Keep watching."

Jack groaned and stretched his aching bones. "Jeez, I feel old. How long are we going to wait here?"

"As long as it takes," she responded unsympathetically.

"What exactly are we waiting for?

"I don't know, to be honest."

She started fiddling with the mobile and dialled a few numbers. "The bugs seem to be working."

"Can you hear anything?"

"Nothing, but he's alone. He'd hardly be talking to himself."

This felt as if it could be a long night, so Jack shuffled into a gap between two rough limestone outcrops and they sat in silence, until nature flicked a switch and, save for an outside lamp hanging from the wall of the villa and a light far out to sea, all was dark.

The sky was clear and now dotted with stars, and although some residual heat of the day remained, it was fleeing fast, and he doubted that his clothing would comfortably see him through the night.

"How cold does it get at night in these parts?" he asked.

"Eighteen, nineteen."

"It feels colder."

Amanda didn't seem to care. "We'll need to take turns here – say an hour at a time."

Jack said, "Are stakeouts usually this boring?"

"Yes, and uncomfortable. Just keep watching."

So that's what he did, the only action he observed being the sensible withdrawal of Chandler from the patio into the house. More moaning was pointless, so he prepared himself instead for a long, cold vigil. "How long since you've done this?"

She made to answer but stopped, her senses alert.

From a distance and in a direction of which he could not be sure, the low drone of a car intruded into the silence. The drone persisted, then grew louder and, a few seconds later, the red tail lights of the vehicle passed close beside them and turned into the narrow track which led to Chandler's villa.

The car halted, and a moment later the courtyard of the villa was illuminated by powerful lamps as Chandler emerged. The gates swung open. The car circled, then halted in the courtyard, and when Chandler had returned from the gates to the house, the car driver had emerged, and the two men shook hands - all the time Amanda's camera capturing the scene.

The visitor was older and not as tall as Chandler, with short, curly hair gradually losing its grip on his skull. He was dressed casually, and, after the men had engaged in a short conversation, they disappeared inside the villa.

Jack turned to Amanda. "Who's that?"

"That's Frank Connor."

Jack whistled inaudibly. "Did you expect him?"

"Not exactly, but I thought it possible."

She lit a torch, carefully wedged it between two rocks to allow discreet lighting and again began fiddling with the phone. She hit the speaker and they leant towards it.

Jack laughed. "Is this the best MI5 can do?"

"Pretty much in the time we had."

Voices came through, amazingly loud and clear.

"Works quite well, so just listen."

Jack didn't feel so cold now, and they both listened to a story which was well worth listening to.

Chapter 42

Frank Connor drank two long mouthfuls of whisky, placed down the empty tumbler on the heavy glass table, then looked across at the British Prime Minister. The men were about the same age, but he knew that Adam Chandler looked about ten years younger and he envied him his unruffled face and handsome features.

Connor had long given up kidding himself that his was an attractive face, and he wondered whether if he had been similarly blessed, his life would have taken a different path. In his profession, looks just didn't matter and could never substitute for brains.

Chandler said, "So how are you, Frank? We didn't really get a chance to talk last time."

"I'm tired, Adam. Very tired. Ready to move on."

"On to what?"

"I'm not exactly sure. Somewhere quiet and peaceful and away from everyone, especially my colleagues."

"And it's that simple, to just step off the merry-go-round, to just retire?"

Connor said, "Not simple, but we've all got to retire some time, Adam. I'm not expecting a leaving gift and a speech from colleagues in the office canteen."

He paused, maybe waiting for a laugh, but Chandler wasn't laughing. "So how does this all work?"

Connor said, "Assure me that our goods will arrive as arranged, give me the money and I go."

Chandler lit a cigarette. "What if I don't pay?"

"Now, Adam, why would you not pay? You like being prime minister and I want you to stay prime minister. For what it's worth, I think you're doing a grand job. Now, why would you want to spoil everything? Besides" – and Connor's eyes narrowed a little – "not to pay would be very foolish."

"The goods will be in transit soon."

"Dates, times and places as agreed?"

"Yes."

"So that just leaves the money?"

Chandler reached down to the side of the sofa and produced a large holdall, which he handed across to Connor.

Connor sat it on his lap and looked inside. He was a very experienced man in dealing with large amounts of cash, the products of many fundraising bank heists. He emptied the holdall onto the glass table and arranged it carefully. He picked up a few random bundles and flicked through pristine hundred-pound notes. "A lot of money, Adam, but my guess is that we're a bit short of five million. Do I need to count it again?"

Chandler said, "Impressive. There is precisely £4,850,000."

"So, where's the rest?"

"There is no rest. Do you imagine I can just walk into the Royal Mint or the treasury and walk out again with five million pounds? It's all I've got and then some, and if it's not enough, well, there it is. I'm not wealthy, Frank. Politics in Britain doesn't pay that well."

Connor looked at him hard and said coldly, "Adam, we both know you've been on the take for years."

"Look, that's all I've got, except for about £1,000 in a current account." Chandler laughed and added, "Mind you, I get paid on Friday."

Connor's face broke into a smile. He reached into the holdall, carefully extracted several bundles of notes and threw them carelessly onto the table. "I'm not a greedy man, Adam. Four and a half million will do me nicely for the remainder of my days. Take this and don't spend it all at once."

Chandler looked at the money and then at Frank Connor. "And that's it?"

"Yes, Adam, that's it."

Chandler rose from the sofa and poured two drinks, gave one to Connor, then resumed his seat on the sofa.

Connor threw across a small buff folder. "Witness statements and logs, all originals."

Chandler opened the folder. "No copies?"

"You have my word."

"And only you know the whole story?"

"Now that my sister's gone, it's just me."

"Sorry, I didn't know."

"Why would you, Adam?"

Chandler laid the folder down. "So only you know the full story now?"

"First hand, I suppose so."

"And I have the documents, and you're here alone."

"Don't be silly, Adam," Connor said complacently. He clasped the holdall tightly and emptied his drink. "I need to be going now. Don't bother to see me out. I'll be seeing you."

Chapter 43

The door slammed. Chandler shut his eyes and breathed heavily. It was over.

He made his way back to the drinks trolley and poured a large one. The door clicked open.

Frank Connor was back, this time not alone.

They made a strange trio. Connor looked much the same, but Chandler detected that his airy self-confidence had certainly gone and he wore an expression, if not of fear, then something close to it.

He was staring ahead at Chandler, but this time he was not giving the instructions.

On Connor's right, Sheila Cahill wore a business suit totally unsuited to the Maltese evening. Alongside her was a tall, powerfully built man. He spoke first. "Well, Sheila, are you going to introduce us?"

"Adam, this is Patrick Lawrence. He's a journalist."

Patrick Lawrence said, "Of course, Sheila can't introduce our friend here." He looked menacingly at Connor. "Sheila, let me introduce an old friend of mine – Frank Connor."

"Patrick, it's probably best if Mr Connor leaves us," and Sheila added intimately, "We have our business to attend to."

Lawrence said, "Oh, business – business can wait a minute. Let's all have a drink."

Cahill seemed about to protest, but Lawrence said, "How about a drink, Mr Chandler? What will you have, Frank? Sheila?"

Chandler gave a shrug and moved to the drinks trolley. He mixed the drinks and handed each one of them a glass in turn.

Lawrence said, "Cheers," and the others raised their glasses silently.

Lawrence let out a long sigh of satisfaction at a thirst sated and said, "Why don't we go out onto the patio? It's a beautiful evening."

No one demurred, and they trudged out, again in silence, and sat on the chairs around the round wooden table on the cliff edge patio. Only distant waves lapping against the limestone cliffs broke the silence of the night.

Lawrence sat at the head of the table. "Lovely place you've got here, Adam. Terrific place for a quiet weekend."

Chandler said, "Yes, it usually is."

Lawrence laughed. "Yes, we have rather disturbed things for you; however, there's no sense in ruining the entire weekend. Now, Sheila, you have business with the prime minister. Will you start?"

Cahill said, "Time yet, Patrick. We don't want to bore Mr Connor. Let's enjoy our drinks first."

Lawrence was certainly enjoying his drinks and went for another, this time returning with the bottle of gin. "Sheila, I'm sure Frank doesn't mind, and it might be useful. He's in the same business as me."

Connor gave a watery smile, but it was now the turn of Chandler to go deadly white.

Cahill said firmly, "Look, Patrick, we don't need another journalist."

Lawrence laughed. "Maybe not, but let's just start. Frank's going nowhere. You don't mind, Adam? I mean, if Frank stays?"

Chandler was too white to respond, and Lawrence turned his attention to Connor. "Good, that's all settled."

Cahill tried again. "I really think it would be better if Mr Connor left now."

Lawrence ignored this, but Cahill had had enough and decided to put him in his place. "Look, Patrick, just shut up. This is my show. Mr Connor obviously doesn't want to stay and we don't need him here."

Lawrence again demurred, this time with decisive effect. "He's staying, Sheila." He reached into his leather coat and produced a gun, which he looked at keenly from a number of angles before laying it on the table in front of him.

The appearance of the gun drew a shriek from Cahill.

"Let's just start, Sheila."

Cahill's eyes widened and a look of fear and bemusement broke across her face. She looked at Lawrence, Chandler, then back at the gun.

"Start," Lawrence repeated.

Cahill said, "Well, Adam, I came to see you because of this note." She threw it across the table.

Chandler glanced at it, "Well, you could have saved yourself a trip because it's a load of nonsense. Surely this could have waited until Monday?"

"No, it can't wait, because in following up this note I've been made aware of further information and serious allegations. I can go over them if you like, but the bottom line is that it would be best for the party if you considered your position."

Chandler laughed weakly.

Connor said, "Why should Adam resign because of an anonymous note? I expect politicians receive a varied post bag?"

Cahill said confidently, "Well this note is pretty much true, but that's really not so important, given where it's led me." She stared at Chandler. "I have details of the affairs, of course, but also bribes to keep secrets and payments for favours. We can go through all of them if you like, but resignation is your only option. Of course, if we can agree the transitional arrangements, it might be that all this needn't come out."

"Yet you have a journalist with you, Sheila," Chandler retorted.

"I have not shared the detailed information – yet."

She paused, possibly for effect. Everyone laughed.

Connor was still laughing, "Sorry, Miss Cahill. I'm afraid that you and Mr McMahon got this all wrong."

Cahill was white. "How do you know about McMahon?"

Connor shrugged.

Cahill said shrilly, "Look, I've got everything. Christ, I've got a recording of Adam and McMahon agreeing pay-off terms."

Chandler's head was shaking continually now.

Cahill's voice had raised an octave. "Are you not listening? I've got a recording."

Lawrence said, "Shut up, you silly bitch, that's not McMahon on the tape."

Cahill stammered, "How do you know who it is?"

Lawrence didn't speak, but his gaze rested on Connor.

"What's it got to do with him?" Cahill asked.

Connor admitted, "It's got everything to do with me, but you're not completely wrong, Miss Cahill. Adam will be paying for silence, but to me and certainly not to you."

Cahill looked hopeless now. "Patrick?"

Lawrence contributed a sneer and Connor continued casually, "Your further researches are interesting, I congratulate you. I really didn't think you would do so well. Of course, I couldn't be sure of that at first."

Cahill was wilting in the face of the reality of power. There was nothing to spin any more; there were just facts. "What does that mean?"

It was just business to Connor. "Well, I had to kill a few people as insurance, you see." He looked at Chandler, whose eyes now faced the floor. "I couldn't risk anyone else destroying him, because I need him where he is. You see, Adam's no use to me or my organisation without power. That's all that really matters. As it turned out, I needn't have bothered – the note was all wrong. You were all wrong. If only you hadn't been so sure of yourself, they might have lived.

However, you did eventually find out some things that I would rather you hadn't. Anyway, I had to protect my investment."

Cahill said, "You killed Allardyce and Patterson?"

Connor said, "Don't forget Mr McMahon."

Cahill's mouth opened again, but no sound came out.

"So, yes, I am responsible for these deaths, although I didn't kill them with my own hands. You see, Miss Cahill, the organisation I represent has many volunteers."

Connor indicated with a hand and a mock bow. "And Patrick is one of our bravest and finest. With your information he handled the business end of the operation. I'm afraid you picked the wrong journalist, Miss Cahill."

Cahill was shaking now and barely able to control her voice. She turned slowly to the man at her side and asked desperately, "Patrick?"

He looked at her with cold dead eyes but didn't say anything, instead returning Connor's bow.

She asked again in a shrill pleading tone, "Patrick?"

Lawrence was still looking at Connor. "Shut up, Sheila. I'm warning you now. Not another word."

Cahill just couldn't stop. "Patrick, tell me this is all nonsense."

His lips remained closed.

Cahill rose from the table and looked again at Lawrence, then at Chandler. With an effort she summoned a measure of control, "I'm not listening to any more of this. I'm going back to the hotel."

Lawrence said, "You're going nowhere. Now sit fucking down. Now!"

She turned on her heel but, as she did so, Lawrence grabbed her wrist.

She screamed, "Get away from me, Patrick. I'm not listening to another word."

Lawrence looked at her moist eyes and, with his hand, flicked her hair back off her face. He spoke softly now. "Sit down, Sheila."

She mumbled an incoherent protest. A protest too far.

In a single movement, Lawrence wrapped his powerful arms around her, lifted her almost over his head and walked a few paces. He took care to halt before the low chain guard, then despatched the spin doctor over the barrier into the blackness.

Chapter 44

Lawrence returned to his seat. Chandler put his hands over his bowed head, and Connor's expression was unchanged.

Lawrence poured himself another drink and lit a cigarette. "Well, Frank, that's all that taken care of. The prime minister's in the clear now – that's what you wanted; that's what you said we needed to do. Keep him in power so he could be useful to our movement." He looked at Connor menacingly. "But of course, you meant useful to yourself, didn't you? You're a traitor, Frank."

Connor said, "Don't call me a traitor, Patrick. I've given everything for this movement, and now I'm done with it. I'm retiring."

Lawrence shook his head. "No, Frank. You betrayed us and you betrayed me. I don't kill people to suit your personal plans, I kill them for a cause." Lawrence curled his fingers round his gun. "So now, Frank, I'm going to kill you for a cause."

Connor was calm. "Patrick, put that gun down. You're not going to kill me."

Lawrence raised the gun.

Connor continued blandly, "You see, Patrick, killing me won't help the cause; it'll damage it, perhaps beyond repair."

"Killing traitors never weakens us, Frank. You taught me that."

Connor lit a cigarette. "Before your untimely arrival, my deal with Adam was that I got a month's start, and I want that from you as well.

Once I'm out of the way, there's no risk to the movement. But, Patrick, if I don't make the month, then it's all over. I've got maps of every arms dump, records on every cell, every volunteer in Ireland, Scotland, England and the United States. I've got bank account numbers and the whole money trail. If I don't make the month, and I don't check in every day, then they're all on their way to MI5."

The gun still pointed at Connor, but Lawrence's finger was off the trigger now.

"Besides which, Patrick, I'm leaving the organisation with a source of arms for many years. It's all arranged, thanks to Adam."

Lawrence took a long drag on his cigarette. He replaced his gun on the table and looked at Connor. "And after a month, what then?"

"All the papers get destroyed; all the names forgotten."

"How do we know that?"

"You can trust me, Patrick."

Lawrence said, "You wouldn't be bluffing would you, Frank?"

Connor's face was impassive.

"No, of course you're not." Lawrence extended his hand and they shook. "After a month, we'll come after you, Frank."

"I know you will, Patrick."

Lawrence said, "But tell you what, Frank: tell me what you've got on this bastard, and I promise we'll leave you be. You can keep the money, clear off, do what you say with the documents. Tell me about Chandler, and there'll be no one after you."

Connor considered. "Well, that might work." He looked at Chandler, who looked desperate. "It would be nice not to have to look over my shoulder for the rest of my life."

It was the easiest decision of Connor's life. He shook his head. "Sorry, Patrick, I have already given Adam my word, so I can't do that. I guess I'll just have to take my chances."

Lawrence shrugged. "Honourable to the end, Frank. Have it your way." He picked up his gun and put it back in his jacket.

Chapter 45

When the second car had arrived at Chandler's villa, Amanda had decided to abandon the high ground and to close the distance between themselves and the villa. Although the courtyard was still illuminated, the ground leading to the residence was not, and Jack had stumbled and fallen several times, cursing loudly.

Once at the gates, they had tried to watch and listen to the company, but the intermittent whistles of wind off the ocean interfered with the ability to form the overheard words into a coherent message. In response, Amanda had slipped the bolt of the gate and they had moved through, eventually ending up just behind the gable wall, in complete darkness and only a few yards from Chandler and his guests.

Jack had stood behind Amanda and had found it almost impossible to stay still and quiet, but somehow, he had managed. Only once had he reacted, an automatic reflex as they had watched Lawrence despatch Cahill over the cliff edge, but he had been checked by Amanda. There was no way they could have saved her, and he understood that they needed to get the whole story, which they now had.

Now Amanda had the Glock in her hand raised to the sky. She put her mouth to his ear. "Get out your gun and back me up. Cover Connor."

Jack nodded. Out came the gun. His hand shook.

Amanda moved half a step forward and took a last look. Lawrence and Connor had their backs to them about four or five strides away, with Chandler facing but staring into space.

Jack's heart was thumping. He wasn't sure whether his legs would support him, but Amanda didn't give him long to worry about that. She sprang forward and stopped behind Patrick Lawrence with her gun pressed to the nape of his neck.

Jack flicked his eyes between the other two men. Chandler, although he started, was certainly not a threat. Connor was alert, but his face remained impassive and his hands made no movement as Jack pointed his gun at him.

Amanda said to Lawrence, "Slowly open your coat – not another movement." Lawrence did as he was told, and Amanda reached inside his coat and removed his gun. She turned to Connor. "Have you got a gun?" Connor smiled and slowly opened his arms. She declined the offer to search him.

It wasn't even worth searching Chandler. She said to him, "Where's the dossier that Mr Connor gave you?"

Chandler mumbled, "Inside, on the table, buff folder."

Amanda said, "Jack, go and get that."

He was back quickly, and he handed it to Amanda, who was now sitting pointing her gun at Lawrence.

She introduced herself while leafing through the file, all the time rapidly flashing her eyes to each man in turn.

Connor said. "Well, Miss Barratt, what now?"

"Mr Connor, as everyone else is making deals, let me propose another."

"I'm listening."

"It seems to me that you've got everything I need. I've got the dossier on the prime minister, but I'm greedy. I want everything. The records on your organisation. Give that to me and answer a few of my questions and you can go."

"Simple as that."

"Yes."

Connor said, "With the money?"

Amanda shrugged. "Yes. It's all dirty money."

"And if I don't?"

"Maghaberry Prison, just outside my home town. But don't worry, it'll just be a short sentence, because I'm going to get the paperwork all wrong. An unfortunate bureaucratic blunder and there you are on the wrong wing."

"Your home town?" Connor said.

"I'm a Lisburn girl."

"Not my kind of town."

Amanda said, "I'm going to have about a dozen policemen here in five minutes."

Lawrence, unblinking, stared at Connor. A hard face, a face full of hate. "Careful, Frank."

Connor smiled.

Lawrence stood up.

Amanda said, "Sit down, Mr Lawrence."

Jack backed off a pace, unsure what to do. But he was slow, an amateur in a deadly professional game, and while he was thinking about it, Lawrence's arm came crashing down on his wrist. The pain was acute, and although he tried not to, he dropped the gun.

Lawrence bent down, then picked it up in a single elegant movement and turned to face Amanda, a smiling killing machine, and he was still smiling when the girl from Lisburn put a bullet in his brain and then double-tapped the gun, delivering two more bullets which ripped through his chest. Lawrence gave the world a last smile and fell to the ground.

Amanda leant over him and, seemingly satisfied, handed Jack his gun. "Try to keep a hold of this, please."

She returned to her seat. "Now, Mr Connor, I've made things a bit easier for you."

"You mentioned questions, Miss Barratt."

"How did Mr Lawrence kill Allardyce, Patterson and McMahon?"

"Easily, it's what he does."

"He did it very well. I haven't got a shred of evidence."

"Ah, Miss Barratt. That's what you should expect with Patrick. He killed people easily. He didn't favour guns. It was all very simple with him. He was the best I've ever seen, and I've known a lot of killers. They called him the Ghost." Connor reflected, "You killed a legend, Miss Barratt."

Amanda ignored this dubious honour. "Did he kill David Ross and my agent at the nursing home?"

Chandler lifted his head and finally spoke. "David's dead?"

Amanda said, "Yes, as if you give a shit."

Chandler started to mumble something.

Amanda said, "Shut up, prime minister. I'm talking to Mr Connor."

"But ..."

"But nothing." She didn't look at him but hit him a backhand blow which caught him flush in the cheek. Chandler yelped out a protest. Jack wasn't convinced that she ought to be doing that to the prime minister, but in fairness it shut him up. She turned back to Connor. "What about it, Mr Connor? Did you arrange to kill Ross and my agent?"

"No. I don't know who Ross is. It seems that Mr Ross is Adam's business."

Amanda tightened her lips but decided not to pursue this. "And the details of your organisation?"

"I'm not carrying that with me, you'll need an email address."

"MI5 can manage that."

She took out her phone and dialled a number. "Max?"

She threw the phone across to Connor. "Speak to my colleague, Mr Connor."

This didn't take long and Connor handed the phone back to Amanda. "Thanks, Max." She turned to Connor. "Time for you to leave."

Jack turned in response to a low sound. Over the hills, lights were flickering. Cars were approaching, very near now.

Chapter 46

Exhaustion, possibly due to the ebbing of his weekend adrenaline, was mostly what Jack felt as he drank coffee after coffee while lying comfortably on the sofa in Amanda's Bloomsbury office. Amanda, on the other hand was still busy. Nowhere near finished. How did she do it?

She ended a testy-sounding phone call, then Max Harris came into the office. "Here's that report you wanted on these companies. And the analysis of that phone you picked up at the cottage hospital."

Amanda tensed. "Any link?"

"Yes, a single incoming call."

Amanda leant back in her chair. "Thanks, you can clear off now if you want. Have a few days off."

Harris nodded, but he didn't leave the office. "Can I have a word, boss?"

"Of course. Do you want me to kick Jack out?"

"No, leave him. He looks comfortable."

Jack grunted his thanks.

Harris said, "I've been thinking about Emma."

"Me too," Amanda said.

"I know you have. She and I both loved working for you. Do you know why?"

No one could answer that question.

"It's not that you're brilliant."

"Thanks for that."

"Sorry, I mean you are great at your job, but it's more than that, Emma, and me as well, we're young but not stupid. Maybe it's naïve, but everyone here believes in you. Believes that you're honest and you'll do the right thing. I don't know what the right thing is, but, well, you get it right most of the time. That's important to me, and it was important to Emma."

Amanda said, "Having your confidence is important to me."

"You have it. It's everything really. Working for MI5 can be morally challenging. We break the law, we snoop, we have power and can destroy lives. If you can't believe that you're doing this for the greater good then, I mean, who could do it?"

Amanda said, "I agree with you. You know that."

"Yes, I know, but there is one thing. Not about the people that we catch, but the people that we don't."

"We can't clear up everything."

"I know that. I'm thinking about the ones we could stop but don't. Political considerations. It sometimes seems that it's the most powerful people that get the benefit of the doubt."

"Sometimes that happens," Amanda admitted.

"Oh, I know it has to happen sometimes, but I'd hate to think that anyone involved with killing Emma gets away."

"Emma's killer is dead."

"And no one else was involved?"

"I'm still looking into that."

"Does that report help?"

"Yes, it does."

Max said, "If there is someone else, will you make sure they are brought to justice?"

Jack was sitting up now. What a question.

"I'll do my best," Amanda said.

"Good enough for me, boss."

He shut the door as he left. Amanda put her head in her hands and rubbed her eyes vigorously.

Jack said. "Tough at the top?"

"It's tougher at the bottom, but yes, that was an interesting meeting."

"As I already told you, you can't quit."

"Maybe not. Funnily enough, I was speaking to my boss a minute ago about exactly these sorts of moral dilemmas."

"It sounded a difficult call."

"Not difficult. Nick Devoy's great. He left things to me. He always backs me. I have no idea what will happen when he leaves."

"Is he leaving soon?"

"Yes, this year sometime."

Jack relapsed in the sofa. "Another coffee?"

"No, we've got things to do."

Chapter 47

Throughout the drive of about two hours, Jack had asked Amanda nothing and she had volunteered the same, so he slept a little.

There weren't many boats in the harbour and very little activity. The water looked choppy.

Jack said, "Where are we?"

"Weymouth."

They got out of the car.

"Put that on," Amanda said.

Body armour. Great.

"I'll get you a gun when we get on board, but don't worry – it's just a precaution."

"I've heard that before."

She smiled. "Come on. Our taxi will be here soon."

He followed her to the quayside and lit a cigarette. The wind was strong. This was worrying.

"How long?"

"A few minutes." She pointed out to sea. "That's our boat."

A grey blue boat (or was it a ship?) was approaching. Jack pointed. "Yes, that's it."

"It looks like a mini warship."

"Something like that. One of our HMCs."

"And that stands for?"

"Her Majesty's Cutter. Our Border Force use them. They're Home Office as well."

"And you can summon them up?"

"For something important, yes."

"Are they fast?"

"Yes, very and, you'll be pleased to know, pretty good on rough seas."

"I am pleased to know that. Where are we going?"

"A pleasant cruise on the channel."

"Would a life jacket not be better than body armour?"

"That depends. Are you okay?"

"Yes fine."

Her Majesty's Cutter proved to be fast and manoeuvrable, and with little fuss they were on board and heading out of the harbour. They were ushered up some metal steps and into a control room.

Amanda shook hands with a powerful-looking individual. She looked at Jack and back at the man. "Commander Tom Phillips, this is Jack Edwards."

Mutual nods were exchanged and Phillips returned to what seemed an impossibly complex mash of technology.

"Have a look at this." Amanda beckoned Jack alongside.

The English Channel was a busy place. "Busiest shipping lane in the world," Phillips said with a suspicion of pride.

Amanda said, "Any word from Portsdown?"

"Yes, good and bad news."

"The good news?"

"It's a fishing boat, easy to interdict – that is, if we can catch it. It's heading for the Irish box."

"Dunlough Bay?"

"Maybe. Is there an Irish connection, or is that classified?" Phillips asked.

"There is a connection, but as for this operation, I was never here."

"Oh, that sort of classified?"

"Afraid so. So how long to interception?"

"That depends on sea conditions, but it could be a long night. And we could breach the Irish twelve-mile limit. I suppose letting them in on the secret is out of the question?"

"Sorry."

Conditions on-board were a little better than Jack anticipated, and after the short meeting with Phillips, they repaired to a small but well-appointed kitchen area. The coffee was good, freshly ground from a shiny, spluttering and expensive-looking machine. Jack couldn't work that out either, but he decided not to try, preferring instead to ask about everything else that he hadn't understood.

"I've got questions."

"Shoot."

"So, we're tracking a boat. How do we know what boat to track?"

Amanda smiled. "A very good question. We'll make an investigator of you one day. The truth is that I've been lucky at last. You remember Hugh?"

"Yes, your retired field man."

"That's him. Well, he caught up with Frank Connor just as he was leaving his house. He followed him south to a harbour where he parked up. Then Connor went for a stroll, and Hugh saw him making a dead drop. You know what that is?"

"I think so."

"Good. Hugh waited then investigated the package. Cash, twenty or so thousand pounds."

"A lot of money. Did he confiscate it?"

Amanda sighed. "Of course not. He waited."

"And?"

"A woman picked it up."

"And the woman was?"

"She works at the port. A night shift controller and co-ordinator, responsible for, among other things, feeding in details of vessel movements to Maritime Security Agencies."

Jack said, "So, she's going to turn a blind eye to a particular vessel."

"Very good."

"I still can't work out how you know which vessel."

"Obviously the one that she doesn't record and doesn't show up in the system."

"But if it's not in the system?"

"We have our own independent system. It's a simple subtraction."

"Okay, I get that. What's the Irish box?"

"A marine area, a sort of rectangle south of Ireland."

"And Dunlough Bay?"

"West of Ireland is a traditional smuggling area."

"It sounds like a good job, but why not just call the Irish Navy. Do they have one?"

"Yes, they do, but it's pretty small. Unfortunately, with operations like this it's never wise to share information. Major smuggling operations nearly always have a body on the inside, and we know for sure there's at least one in this case, and probably more."

"Why do you say that?"

"Twenty thousand can buy more than one person."

"Yes, I see. What about this twelve-mile limit?"

Amanda laughed. "That bit might be risky."

"A risk of a diplomatic incident?"

Her voice was hard now. "That is a risk, but these guns won't be getting landed, I can assure you of that."

Jack said, "It seems crazy that guns are going here anyway. Didn't all the guns get scrapped years ago?"

"The oldest ones, yes."

"But not all?"

"Not according to our assessments."

"Wasn't there some international folk who said that everything was fine?"

Amanda burst out laughing, and that seemed to close the matter, so Jack relocated to an uncomfortable couch while Amanda delved into a holdall.

She said, "You can take off that body armour. We've got about three hundred nautical miles to go."

Jack sighed. "Estimated time of arrival?"

"Ten hours or so."

The boat listed and rolled. Jack felt a rising wave of nausea. Suddenly, this didn't seem much fun.

Chapter 48

The trip, exciting at first, was now decidedly boring, but after a read of an indifferent novel, some chat, a bit of light sleep and about a dozen cups of coffee, there was at last some activity.

The body armour was back on and Jack was again the reluctant possessor of a Glock 17, the only firearm he could use.

"Don't worry," Amanda said. "It's just a precaution."

"So you said."

"True, but this time it really is a job for professionals only."

"And where are these professionals? I haven't seen anyone."

"Don't worry: they're on board, and they know what they're doing."

Jack said, "I always wondered how one interdicts a boat?"

"I'm a bit hazy on that myself, but trust me – they know what they're doing."

"Let's hope so."

"Let's go and see Phillips."

Philips had a couple of men with him this time. One was focused upon screens and the other, sporting a Heckler and Koch carbine, was in conversation with Phillips.

"Hi, Amanda, this is John Pride, my deputy. He'll lead the boarding party."

Pride said. "Will you be joining us, ma'am?"

"No. Secure the boat, arrest the crew and bring them here. All of them. Then I'll want to have a look around and we'll take it from there."

This order had barely been uttered when Jack recoiled and shut his eyes in response to a blinding light. He cautiously opened his eyes. A foaming sea and a fishing boat, so clear and so close.

Pride had left the cabin and loud voices crackled through a radio. The metal fishing boat lurched wildly, but Phillips was relaxed. Well, he did this every day.

Not much more than ten minutes later, Pride's voice came through clear. "Boat secured, returning to vessel. Crew of six joining us."

Amanda said, "Come on."

Jack followed her and joined Pride on the deck.

"Any good?"

"Amateur hour, ma'am. Crates barely concealed. Three in total. Assault rifles mostly."

"Explosives?"

"I didn't see any."

"Right, I want to have a look."

The fishing boat seemed partially secured, but the swell was violent and irregular, and it required a complex arrangement of ropes and harnesses to ferry them across. They descended some slippery metal steps and emerged into a well-lit hold area with a couple of silent armed guards.

Pride led the way to three crude wooden crates, all of which had been partially prised open.

Jack looked inside. "Is it safe to touch these guns?"

Amanda looked at Pride, who nodded.

Jack lifted a rifle. "AK47?"

Amanda took it from him and lifted it up and down. "Close, AK74, the newer model. It's lighter, among other things."

Pride beckoned her across to another crate, and they conducted an inspection of some metal parts.

Jack said, "What's that?"

Amanda said, "It looks like the parts for a Kord. That's a heavy machine gun." She shook her head and said to Pride, "How long to get these crates across?"

The radio crackled, and Pride started listening. "Understood." Pride turned to Amanda. "The commander has received a communication from an Irish naval vessel. It seems we are within their territorial waters."

"How far away are they?" Amanda asked.

"Fifteen minutes, ma'am."

Amanda moved closer to Pride and spoke in his ear. He dismissed the guards.

Amanda and Pride worked quickly, fiddling with each crate in turn while Jack watched on.

"Time to go," Amanda said.

After an equally difficult return, at least for Jack, they headed back to the bridge of the Cutter in time to recoil against a violent acceleration of the craft. The spotlights were off now and everything was dark.

Phillips said, "Sixty seconds, ma'am."

Jack counted in his head until Phillips said, "Out of Irish territorial waters now."

Amanda grabbed Jack's arm and led him outside.

Everything was black. Salty spray wet his face. "What's up? I can't see a thing."

She didn't reply, just kept a tight hold of him, compelling him to look ahead into the blackness until a flash of yellow white light and, a few seconds later, a deafening blast left Jack in no doubt about the fate of the fishing boat.

Chapter 49

In Lord North Street, central London, close to the end of the working day, Jack struggled to keep up with Amanda and four suited agents as she strode through an imposing wooden door and into a large open-plan office area.

There was only a single desk, but all around a dizzying array of communications equipment. All the screens were blank.

A brunette woman of about thirty, sporting a number of designer labels, looked up calmly. "Can I help you?"

Amanda flashed her card. "Mr Slater, please."

"Please give me a moment. We are a little disarranged. We seem to have lost power."

"Yes, I've cut the power. Is Mr Slater in the office?"

The woman stopped and looked at Amanda, "Why did you cut the power?"

"That's really nothing to do with you. Are you Samantha Frost?"

"Yes."

Amanda indicated to one of her men. "Take her away."

This was a shock to Jack, but it was more of a shock to Samantha Frost, who now abandoned her crisply cut vowels and perfectly composed grammar.

Amanda laughed. "So much for breeding."

Jack had questions but there was no time, and he followed on as she crashed through another door.

There were two men in the office sitting behind an imposing desk. Each cast hostile looks at Amanda. She flashed her card again and pulled a couple of chairs roughly alongside the desk.

Bob Slater said, "What do you want, Miss Barratt?"

Amanda ignored him and looked at the other man. "Good afternoon, Julius."

"Hello, Amanda."

Although Jack didn't have a clue what was going on, this was all quite exciting.

Amanda said, "This is Jack Edwards, a colleague. Jack, this is Bob Slater, and Mr Julius Stair, a lawyer. Now why would a lawyer be here? Have you anticipated me, Mr Slater?"

Slater said, "I have no idea what that means."

Stair piped up. "Amanda, my client is quite prepared to assist you with any enquiries that you may have. Surely there's no need for these theatrics?"

Amanda considered this reasonable suggestion. "Shut up, Julius."

Julius Stair, as Jack later learned, was one of the most famous solicitors in London and had represented some of the world's most high-powered accused. He had a reputation to maintain, so he had another go. "I am sure Nick Devoy would prefer any enquiries to be conducted as discreetly as possible."

Amanda said, "I'm fully aware of Nick's views." She turned to Slater. "Mr Slater, I thought you might want news on the prime minister."

Slater did the right thing and said nothing.

"And, of course, the goods that you were importing for him."

Slater shook his head. "I have no idea what you mean."

Amanda said, "There was a difficulty in transit. Rough seas. An accident. I'm afraid the ship was lost, but luckily the crew were saved."

Slater opened his mouth, but in response to a tug on his sleeve shut it again.

"The next thing I'm going to say falls under Official Secrets, so, Julius, if you choose to remain here, you will be bound by the Act, and trust me I'll use all of its provisions against you if you breach it."

All heads turned towards Stair.

"Don't think that you can bully me, Amanda."

"Today I can, Julius, and believe me I will."

This was a lot of pressure to withstand for a man, who, as far as Jack knew, was probably innocent. He wondered what Stair was made of. Slater looked desperate now.

Stair said, "I'm an old man, Amanda, and I know many secrets, official and unofficial. If I don't respect the law now, then what am I?"

A good answer, Jack thought.

Amanda said, "Very well, Julius." She threw a sheet of paper onto the desk. "An affidavit from the prime minister detailing the arms shipment, a few drug shipments and several other corrupt transactions."

Amanda made a token pause, but they were deep into "no comment" territory now. "You're finished, Mr Slater."

She delved into a case and produced another folder. "All the details of the companies involved. All your companies."

Julius Stair said, "My client has a wide range of interests, as you know, Amanda. If any part has broken the law, then my client can hardly be responsible."

Amanda produced more papers. "A statement from David Ross, detailing every transaction between you and Adam Chandler." She reached into her case again, then slammed a small diary so hard on the desk that everyone jumped. "Oh, and Ross's diary. The one you were so anxious to get."

Stair recovered first. "Obviously, there are serious issues to be discussed here. I think the time has come to make things formal. Do you intend to charge my client with something?"

"I don't charge people, that'll be for others, but I anticipate this will happen."

"Well, I think that you owe my client the courtesy of fully detailing things."

"In due course, perhaps."

Stair looked at her quizzically. "Most unorthodox, Amanda."

"Excuse me a moment." With this, Amanda left the office. This left Jack and the two men sitting in silence. For fifteen minutes, Jack knew the meaning of the word uncomfortable.

The door opened. Amanda's face was neutral. She sat down slowly.

Everyone waited.

Amanda said, "Sorry, I'm waiting for one more phone call."

Stair said, "This is becoming surreal. Can I telephone Nick Devoy?"

Amanda smiled sweetly. "I've already told you once to shut up, Julius. For the record, you can't phone Nick, you can't phone anyone."

Her mobile rang. Everyone listened as Amanda said yes twice and then thank you.

She said, "Samantha's talking. Singing like a canary, as they say in the movies, Mr Slater. Poor girl, she's got no choice really. I've got her calls and bank transfer to your assassin: that's the lady who's lying in our morgue. A full statement, they tell me. Unbreakable. I'm sure you know how efficient Samantha is."

Slater shut his eyes, breathed in heavily and cast a long silent appeal to Stair, but nothing came back.

Stair said, "I must insist that I am allowed to call Nick Devoy."

"You can insist all you fucking want, Julius. Do you think I'd be doing this if Nick Devoy didn't have my back?"

She turned to Slater. "Some things we can talk about, even let go. It would have been a stretch to overlook a major drug deal which financed terrorism, or even an illegal arms shipment, but stranger things have happened. But, Mr Slater, nobody gets to kill one of my agents."

Chapter 50

Frank Connor had led an extraordinary life. Every day for close on fifty years, his nerves pulsating, every minute anticipating death. But it hadn't come to him, just to other people. He felt different today, calmed by the gently lapping water of the Black Sea.

He opened his eyes and sighed with satisfaction. A beautiful day with an endless azure blue sky and gently lapping water. Beauty had always been important to Connor. He had seen and touched so much horror, that without beauty, he could never have gone on.

But he had gone on. For many decades, as leader one of the world's most effective paramilitary forces. He had never questioned the justice of its cause, nor the necessity of its methods.

Most described him as ruthless, a man without heart or pity, but they were wrong. Connor was just consistent. He knew in his heart that he had never ordered or engaged in any activity that he did not believe was best for the organisation. There had been times when what was right and what was wrong had been a difficult call, but Connor always decided, acted and then moved on.

Now it was all over. He allowed himself a few recollections. Back to that hot night so many summers ago. A long council meeting and, at last, home to the little terraced house – and Mary. She always smiled when she saw him and she would pour him tea as they sat for hours around a small fire, absorbed in each other's, often silent, company.

But that evening, when he had opened the door and hung up his coat in the hall, she had not responded to his hail.

The giant teapot was on the fireplace and the table furnished with the little china cups. All in the room was undisturbed, save for the carpet upon which his beloved Mary lay on her back, still with a smile on her saintly face but with what was undeniably an ear-to-ear wound cut deep into and across her neck.

Connor's detached discipline had been tested as never before that day, but even then, in the face of such a personal catastrophe, he had stayed true to the principle of organisation first. No precipitate retaliation, just a quick efficient investigation and identification of the assassins. He had killed them, of course, but only after thoroughly establishing that their elimination was essential to the interests of the organisation. It was for cold-blooded, unemotional decisions such as this that Connor was feared and why he had retained his leadership for so long.

With Mary gone, he had vowed never to love again, and in this Connor had kept his word.

Then, a powerful thought of his brother – his dead brother. Jimmy had protected him at school, slipped him money when he could and introduced him to the organisation.

But Jimmy had been weak. Once, desperate for money, he had sold a piece of low-level intelligence. Low-level or not, standing orders were standing orders. Frank himself had delivered the summary judgement. It had broken his sister's and mother's hearts, and although no words were ever spoken, Connor knew that they knew. The hurt between them lasted until the day they had died.

There were other mothers and sisters, dozens, maybe hundreds, who last remembered their loved ones as distorted, often dismembered cadavers. Connor acknowledged that he could never understand the depths of their grief. Policemen and soldiers, some who deserved death and some who didn't.

He wondered where the souls of the dead were now, and whether they were at peace.

At least he was at peace now. A peace that comes when you know that the past can never be undone, and you have spent all of your energy on behalf of your cause. It was true that some information had to be given up in exchange for retirement, but the organisation would recover and the armaments would bestow a long-term advantage.

Only the present mattered and everything was perfect. This country was cheap, and his new house and private beach hadn't made a dent in his retirement fund. He leant back in his lounger. Lunch was still half an hour away. A small fishing boat drifted across the horizon and he shut his eyes. He loved the beach. The soft sand was perfect in every way, especially in absorbing the sound of footsteps.

Connor was lucky. Dead in an instant.

Chapter 51

It was raining quite hard when Jack and Amanda, arm in arm, walked through a deserted London graveyard. The dead didn't mind the rain and neither did they.

"What you thinking about?" Amanda asked.

"Death, and people with causes."

"Yes, I meet a lot of folks like that, but having a cause doesn't excuse things. Most people's cause is really themselves. It's just the narrative they develop to hide behind and keep themselves sane. If you think about it, all the worst human beings had a cause."

"Don't you have a cause?" Jack asked.

"Of course, but not like Connor and his like."

"Hmm."

"Yes, I suppose it is fairly hypocritical," she conceded, and squeezed his hand.

 But you let Connor go?"

"Well, I got his dossier on the prime minister, and the details of his organisation."

"Is it useful?"

"Yes."

"For finding guns, bombs, that sort of thing."

"A bit, but mostly the names. I've had an interesting morning comparing our notes with it."

"And Chandler, how can you justify keeping him on?"

"Don't worry about him. Someone once said 'in office but not in power'. He's finished. Politically, he's a dead man walking."

"Why not just expose him? Don't you think the public want to know about these things?"

"Possibly."

"And who decides?"

Amanda squeezed his arm. "These are difficult questions. Let's go this way."

"Isn't this place closing soon?"

"It's already closed."

Their feet crunched on the gravel path as they passed endless gravestones, some elaborate, some simple.

"Nearly there."

Amanda led him through a dark avenue, each side lined with burial vaults, the entranceway giving unreadable details of the residents, and a padlocked door a few feet recessed.

"Okay?" she asked.

Jack said, "Yes, I'm fine. I never really objected to graveyards. I'm not sure why. Isn't Karl Marx buried here?"

"On the other side, the East Cemetery. This is the West Cemetery. We've just passed through what's called the Egyptian Avenue and that circular arrangement of vaults just ahead is the Lebanon Circle."

"Seems like I've chosen a good guide," Jack said. "Do you come here often?"

"Actually, I do. I find it peaceful."

"It's certainly that."

"Besides, where else can spies meet in London?"

"I thought that this was a simple romantic walk?"

She kissed him on the cheek. "Well, that as well."

They went up some stone steps, and Amanda stopped in front of a series of vaults. "The catacombs," she said. "We'll wait here."

It wasn't a long wait. Through the evening came the sound of footsteps. Jack looked at Amanda. She had her hand inside her jacket, which wasn't that reassuring.

She smiled. "Don't worry, just force of habit."

An elderly man wearing what looked like gardening clothes emerged and walked towards them.

"Hello, Bernard."

He handed her a small, folded piece of paper, which Amanda read quickly. "Thanks, we'll be leaving in a few minutes."

Chapter 52

Birds chattered and a few squirrels darted up and down trees. Jack and Amanda ambled a few steps until he, spying a lonely bench partly obscured by bowing willow branches, sat down. Amanda brushed off a few leaves and sat alongside him. She said, "Are you going to buy me some dinner tonight?"

"Yes, but I need to know what just happened."

"We can discuss things over dinner."

"No, just for once I want to talk about you. Maybe you and me. I'm sick of talking about people like Chandler. One day he'll be buried in a fashionable place like this and folks on guided tours will stop and look at his stone. Chattering about him and famous people. There are seven and a half billion people in the world, and Chandler's worse than nearly all of them."

"Forget about it. He'll get what he deserves. These thoughts can drive you crazy. Besides, I thought you believed in eternal justice?"

"I do."

"Well, that's all right then."

"I suppose so."

"So, what about that dinner?"

"What was that note about?"

"It was about Frank Connor."

"Are you in trouble for letting him go?"

"Hardly, he's dead."

"An accident?"

"No, shot."

"By whom?"

"No one knows. It seems he had taken up residence somewhere in Bulgaria. He was on the beach, beside the Black Sea, and someone shot him. That's all we know officially."

"And unofficially?"

"Ray Dewar's a determined woman."

"Ray Dewar? What are you talking about?"

Amanda said, "They say the power to surprise is good for relationships."

"Well, they were right," he said, slowly turning towards her. "Ray Dewar couldn't kill a fly."

"Don't be so sure. Did you know she's spent her entire life trying to chase down Frank Connor? But it's not so easy to get to someone like that. I think she had given up, but of course when she heard that recording of Chandler and Connor, she recognised his voice instantly."

"Are you going to tell me why?"

"Republican terrorists killed her father. He was a soldier in Northern Ireland. He died when she was a baby."

"And why do you think it was her?"

"I gave her details of Connor's new address."

"How did you know that?"

"Jack, that's what I do."

"You could have signed her death warrant."

"I didn't think so."

"You're crazy. What chance could she have against Connor?"

"Quite a good one, it seems. Connor wasn't protected now, and Ray Dewar's not as feeble as you think. Territorial army reservist and knows how to use a gun."

"I thought you said you wouldn't go after Connor."

"I didn't."

"This is horrifying."

"Why? You've just finished moaning about injustice."

"True, but …"

"But what?"

Jack said, "Are people just pawns?"

"No, but I need to keep asking myself this."

"And what now for Ray Dewar?"

"No idea, but she'll be all right. Are you after her phone number?"

"No, she sounds a bit dangerous."

Amanda said, "And sorry to burst your bubble, she was just hanging around with you to see if she could find out anything about Connor and what he was doing with Chandler."

"Another blow to my conceit." Jack sighed.

"She was too young for you anyway. Besides, you've got me."

He looked at her smiling face. "Have I?"

Amanda walked a slow pace forward. "Do you know what Ross told me?"

"No."

"He said find someone who you can love and who loves you."

Jack's heart thumped. "Have you found someone?"

She brushed some hair off her face and puckered her lips in pantomime fashion.

He moved his lips to hers and touched them softly. Lifting his free arm, he reached his hand to the back of her neck and pulled her towards him. She responded, and it felt good.

They had left the graveyard now and were walking down a narrow lane enclosed by expensive houses.

"Nice houses," Amanda remarked.

"Yes," Jack answered cautiously.

"Don't worry. I'm not going to get all domestic."

Jack wondered if he was worried. He wasn't sure, so he settled for kissing her again, then holding her hand a little tighter. They walked on. He felt strange. Maybe he was happy?

Chapter 53

Adam Chandler knew that you had to be lucky to survive in life and in politics.

There were so many dead, six – or was it seven? A few early morning commuters rushed past. Nobody cared. Why should they? Sixty million died in the world every year. Did that matter? Not much to him.

As for the individuals, Chandler felt nothing.

Frank Connor was a man with a violent past trying to retire. He had died with a bullet in his brain. Karma, most would say.

Bob Slater: his sponsor had everything, they said. Connections right to the top. Untouchable, they said. Not now. No one even knew where he was. Some said Parkhurst, Isle of Wight. Maybe, it would be as good as anywhere. a small cell in a prison full of locked doors and high walls on an island. Who could he speak to and who would listen? Bob was a corrupt man. Now he was finished.

It was a pity about David Ross. David was about the only person he had ever liked, maybe he had even been a friend. Either way he had made a good living out of him, and he was dying anyway.

Amanda Barratt had killed Lawrence. One assassin killing another. Slater had been right about her. Not the usual go-to agent. She had slapped his face. She had the power – for now. One day she too would overreach.

Chandler looked across to the Thames, which was doing what it always did. He bought an ice-cream and reached for his newspaper. Sheila had made the front page. A climbing accident, they said. It was news to him that she had ever climbed, but so what? If it was on the front page, it must be true.

He took out his phone and surfed other tedious headlines. The comments from the great British public were amusing. Pros and cons on Cahill's contribution to public life, a few borderline jokes and a single contributor, a voice in the wilderness, urging unease over three government deaths. A poor tortured man. Getting it right and being labelled a conspiracy theorist for life.

Overall, it was not a bad press for Cahill. Lots of commentators called her Sheila. They liked her. Her last successful spin. If only they had met her, they would have known she had love only for herself. Blinded by arrogance, she was on any measure one of the stupidest people he had ever met. An intellectual they said, yet, without any discernible skills, there was almost nothing that she could do. A champion of causes. All just words.

People were wrong. There weren't infinite realities, just one. Often ugly and always more powerful than anyone could control. You just had to accept that everything was inevitable for humans. There was only the present, and that had to be enjoyed.

He rehearsed his upcoming speech, a form of words re-dedicating himself to public service with an enthusiasm for change. He laughed out loud. Some things were just too funny to keep to yourself.

He threw the newspaper in the bin, leant back lazily on the bench and thought of his single reality – and the big black cloud on his horizon.

But why worry? He couldn't do anything about it, so he would enjoy every minute until the day that Amanda Barratt had no further use for him and released Frank Connor's dossier detailing the killing of a British soldier by a young student thirty years ago.

Jack and Amanda's next adventure will be out soon. Catch up on their earlier cases, by clicking the links below:

The Quartermaster (1)
The Quartermaster: explosive fast moving thriller (Jack and Amanda Thriller Series Book 1) eBook : Parish, Adam: Amazon.co.uk: Kindle Store

Parthian Shot (2)
Parthian Shot: explosive fast moving thriller (Jack and Amanda Thriller Series Book 2) eBook : Parish, Adam: Amazon.co.uk: Kindle Store

Loose Ends (3)
Loose Ends: explosive fast moving thriller (Jack and Amanda Thriller Series Book 3) eBook : Parish, Adam: Amazon.co.uk: Kindle Store

Business as Usual (4)
Business as Usual: explosive fast moving thriller (Jack and Amanda Thriller Series Book 4) eBook : Parish, Adam: Amazon.co.uk: Kindle Store

For latest news, offers and updates and to find out more about Adam Parish visit our website www.adam-parish.com
or follow me at:
Adam Parish Books - Home | Facebook

ENJOY JACKS and KNAVES?

YOU CAN HELP ME WITH JUST A LITTLE MINUTE OF YOUR TIME

If you enjoyed Jacks and Knaves, it would be a great help to me if you could leave a rating with a brief review on Amazon. Most of the major publishers spend a lot of money on marketing. With just a minute of your time, you can give me something special: your support. Many Thanks, Adam

Jacks and Knaves
by
Adam Parish

Book 5 of the
Jack Edwards and Amanda Barratt
Mystery Series

Also by Adam Parish
The Quartermaster (1)
Parthian Shot (2)
Loose Ends (3)
Business as Usual (4)

To sign up for offers, updates
and find out more about Adam Parish
visit our website www.adam-parish.com

Printed in Great Britain
by Amazon